Tate sensed Willow's approach behind him, and inhaled at the press of her body against his back, as if she were bracing him for the changes ahead.

"Murdoch has been your family, even more than your blood family, for many years. It's okay to grieve," she said.

It had been one thing to have Murdoch leave for a while—hard to accept but doable. To know he wouldn't be coming back, would no longer be part of Tate's daily life... That was something for which Tate was completely unprepared.

Closing his eyes, Tate breathed deep and soaked in the heat of Willow against him. Oh-so-slowly her arms moved up his sides to anchor her against his shoulders. Almost as if they were one, braced against the world. As much as he shouldn't want it, he couldn't turn away from the incredible feeling of her melding with him.

When the need grew too strong, he moved toward her instead. Chest to chest. Face-to-face. His hands buried in that fiery hair. He had to have her, had to savor this incredible woman who had come into his life so unexpectedly.

Having made the decision, Tate refused to hurry. If this was the only taste of heaven he ever had, he wouldn't rush it.

* * *

Taming the Billionaire is part of the Savannah Sisters series from Dani Wade!

Dear Reader,

There's nothing like a colorful setting to make a story come alive! I set *Taming the Billionaire* off the coast of Savannah, Georgia, after visiting Tybee Island and Savannah. It's the perfect place for Tate's struggle with the waters that haunt his dreams.

My hero, Tate, is truly an example of enduring the tragedies that life throws at you, then learning to stand up and live again. I was inspired by his struggle to break free from the past. I hope his journey to embrace the present and future is inspiring to you, too!

I love to hear from my readers! You can email me at readdaniwade@gmail.com or follow me on Facebook. As always, news about my releases is easiest to find through my author newsletter, which you can sign up for on my website, www.daniwade.com.

Enjoy!

Dani

DANI WADE

TAMING THE BILLIONAIRE

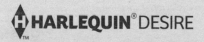

Recycling programs
for this product may
not exist in your area.

ISBN-13: 978-1-335-97139-5

Taming the Billionaire

Printed in U.S.A.

www.Harlequin.com

Dani Wade astonished her local librarians as a teenager when she carried home ten books every week—and actually read them all. Now she writes her own characters, who clamor for attention in the midst of the chaos that is her life. Residing in the Southern United States with a husband, two kids, two dogs and one grumpy cat, she stays busy until she can closet herself away with her characters once more.

Books by Dani Wade

Harlequin Desire

His by Design
Reining in the Billionaire
Unbridled Billionaire
A Family for the Billionaire

Milltown Millionaires

A Bride's Tangled Vows
The Blackstone Heir
The Renegade Returns
Expecting His Secret Heir

Savannah Sisters

Taming the Billionaire

Visit her Author Profile page at Harlequin.com, or daniwade.com, for more titles.

To Charles Griemsman, aka Awesome Editor...
You've taught me a great deal over these years
about writing, communication, story and self-worth.
Thank you for helping me grow in confidence and
style. I'm truly blessed to work with such a kind,
considerate (yet constructive!) editor.

One

Sabatini House. Finally.

Willow stared up at the imposing, impressive castle-like residence through the windshield of her car. The thunderstorm raging around it was only appropriate. A structure as mysterious and unique as Sabatini House deserved an atmospheric introduction.

Unfortunately, since the intercom hadn't worked when she'd stopped at the gates, Willow now had to figure out how to get inside. It took concentrated effort to relax her fingers on the steering wheel.

The rain pounded her little car, at times completely obscuring the view. Willow had been fascinated with Sabatini House for several years, since she'd discovered mention of its owners, the Kingston family, in her great-grandmother's journals. But they contained very little about its history, which had only whetted her appetite for more.

According to the rare articles she'd found about the house since then, it was said to have been built by a Spanish pirate for his lover. It featured underground caves that allowed the ocean to actually flow underneath the house to create a swimming cove. In her journal, Willow's great-grandmother had described the cave from her one and only time sneaking into a party in the house, declaring it a truly magical tie between the land and the sea. As a descendant of pirates herself, that would be something her great-grandmother would have appreciated.

From the outside it still looked like a magnificent castle, with turrets and peaks and arched windows. But Willow was dying for a glimpse of the inside. She hadn't been able to find any photos or documentation in her research. The current reclusive owner had never allowed anyone else inside besides his caretaker, Murdoch Evans, and the occasional trusted workman.

Until today.

Taking a deep breath, Willow pulled her raincoat around her as best she could. There wasn't any point feeling wimpy about the rain. She needed to get inside. The sooner she settled in, the sooner she could start looking for clues. As much as the house fascinated her, the secrets it held were what truly drew her here. Secrets about the Kingstons, and one fateful night generations ago, that could change her own history forever.

Her umbrella would be useless in the strong winds blowing off the water. On the count of three, she jumped out of her car and ran for the side door where Murdoch had told her to enter.

With Murdoch gone to Florida to visit his daughter after she'd had a baby, there was no one to cook and clean for the current resident of Sabatini House. She and Murdoch had gotten to know each other well in the year she'd been pestering him for information about the house. When he'd known he was leaving for the summer, he'd hired her to come in on her summer break from teaching at the local college to take care of the place.

Hiring on without even meeting her employer hadn't seemed that odd at the time. Right about now she was second-guessing that choice.

She'd been due to arrive midafternoon today, but the thunderstorm had blown in early. Packing and driving had become a complicated mess. Living in required she take quite a bit with her, even if she'd be going home to visit on Sundays. Loading the car in the rain had left her and her luggage soggy.

The island would normally have been about a forty-five minute drive from the house where she lived with her sisters in Savannah. Instead she'd been struggling with poor visibility and winds rocking the car for a good hour and a half. So she was now arriving after dark with no warning, since the weather had knocked out the power and phone lines on the island, preventing her from letting her new employer know of the delay.

The rain pelted her with angry pellets as she ran. The flashlight in her hand was her only guide. Reaching the small covered porch was a relief, although not much of one. She fumbled for the key Murdoch had given her.

Excitement shimmered in her belly, even as the effort to get inside exhausted her. She was about to walk into Sabatini House...and hopefully discover all of the mysteries it held.

She knocked hard as she inserted the key and turned it, eager to get out of the rain blowing in under the small porch awning overhead. Giving her new boss a heart attack wasn't on her agenda, but the heavy streaks of lightning splitting the sky didn't encourage her to linger. Fumbling with the keys, flashlight and doorknob, she finally got herself inside and out of the blowing rain. Conscious of the unlit alarm keypad on the wall to her right, she allowed herself to lean back against the now-closed door for only a brief moment. Her heart raced.

"Hello? Mr. Kingston?" she yelled.

Considering the constant barrage of thunder and rain, the odds of him hearing her were slim unless he was close by. She hated to burst in like this, but what other choice had she had? The lines had been down when she'd tried to call earlier in the evening, and there wasn't a cell tower close enough to allow them to work out here. Murdoch had warned her about that. The house was huge, and with the power out there were no lights to guide her.

But that uneasy feeling in the pit of her stomach told her to find him quickly, announce her presence, and make sure he was safe and sound. The fact that he was out here by himself only woke her curiosity. As she tiptoed through the empty room, she wondered where his family was and why he was all alone, even though that was absolutely none of her business.

"Mr. Kingston? It's Willow, your new housekeeper."

Her voice seemed to be swallowed up by the darkness and rain, though the sounds from the storm were muted in this part of the house. The flashlight illuminated the path out of the mudroom where she stood. Thank goodness she'd grabbed a good, sturdy one on her way to the car.

Even inside, the smell of the ocean permeated the air. It mixed with the rain, salty and wet with a slight undertone of some kind of flowers.

She dripped on the tile floor as she made her way through a modernized kitchen, narrow and long like an oversize galley with all the amenities. Murdoch had mentioned the kitchen had been updated about five years ago.

Lightning flashed outside, brightening the entire room through the long row of arched windows along one side. Willow winced, trying to concentrate on her surroundings so she didn't get spooked. Sweeping the flashlight around, she noticed more arches. Every doorway, every window. Some were outlined in brick. Some plaster. Hopefully cleaning the windows wasn't her purview, because there seemed to be a lot of them.

Determining that the room was empty, Willow pushed forward through the kitchen and found a wide hallway at the other end. The whole time she called for Mr. Kingston. The darkness, as well as the thought that he had no idea she was in his house, left her with antsy feet and a churning stomach. And she was increasingly uncomfortable not knowing he was okay.

Hopefully he would forgive her intrusion. Murdoch hadn't said anything about her boss being incapacitated, but in a storm like this anything could happen. A fall. A bad cut. A concussion. All alone, he could lie on the floor injured for hours with no help. He could bleed to death. And there was no way to contact the outside world because the landline was down.

She cautiously made her way down the wide hallway. Everything here was built on a majestic scale. She flicked the beam of light over the various rooms as she went, checking for Mr. Kingston.

Most of the doors were open, some of them revealing empty spaces. Other rooms held furniture covered in sheets. Only a formal living room boasted carefully placed antique furniture, but it still lacked a lived-in look.

If she hadn't known better, and the kitchen hadn't appeared to have been recently used, Willow would have suspected the house was unoccupied. Empty of all life. But she knew Mr. Kingston had to be here somewhere.

Her uneasy feeling grew until Willow's stomach cramped. Yes, the house was huge. Three stories that she knew of, though the turrets suggested more. Still, what more could she do to be heard? The storm seemed to absorb her calls and footsteps.

The hallway finally opened into a large, two-story rotunda-style room centered on an incredible staircase leading upward. The sound of the storm outside now resounded in her ears. The staircase drew her eye as far up as she could see in the darkness. No lights shone on the upper floors, offering no clues as to where her employer might be.

"Mr. Kingston?" she called again, her voice suddenly echoing loudly back from the walls. Guilt snaked through her. Even though she needed him to hear her to answer, it felt wrong to yell in a house that wasn't her own.

A noise, like something small had fallen, barely reached her across the rotunda. "Hello? Is anyone there?"

No response. Only the sound of the rain beating at the house.

Willow swung the flashlight around in a circle, taking note of the numerous doors leading off this room and on the upper floors. A strong sense of uncertainty crept over her. She had no idea where to look, and no idea which direction to go. With this many rooms, she could look all night and possibly never find this man.

Had she made a mistake coming here so late?

Her excitement at finally being inside the house had now given way to more uncertainty, mixed with rapidly rising fear.

A metallic rattle came from the hallway opposite her, ramping her pulse to high speed. Was that a normal noise for the house? She had no idea. Her light reflected back from the ocean-blue tile outlining the bottom of the plaster walls. She took a tentative step forward, struggling to think logically.

The bedrooms were probably upstairs. She'd start on the second floor. He would most likely be there. If she could just find some light. Surely, given how often the power went out on the islands, he would be well equipped with lanterns.

Or a generator. Though if he'd already gone to bed, he might not have bothered starting it. She couldn't remember if Murdoch had mentioned one in his instructions.

Her wet tennis shoes squeaked on the tile as she made her way to the bottom of the staircase. Reaching out, she grasped the wooden balustrade. Her light trailed upward, showcasing the stairs' brilliant blue tiles with a mother-of-pearl glaze. The silver filigree in the blond wooden rail looked delicate but remained firm in her grip. As her light reached the next floor, she caught a shadow move out of the corner of her eye.

Startled, Willow dropped the flashlight from her hand. The clatter echoed through the massive room.

"Hello?" She tried to project her voice, but fear made it tiny. She almost couldn't hear it herself over the rain and rumble of thunder.

Just as she bent forward for the light, a strong arm snaked around her neck, forcing her back against a hard wall of muscle and heat that she recognized as human... and huge.

The size and strength of her attacker told her it had to be a man, but she was too busy trying not to wet her pants to figure out more than that.

The arm around her neck tightened, almost cutting off her air. Then she felt the man's face near hers, his breath harsh in her ear. "Want to explain what you're doing in my house?"

Tate Kingston felt a surge of adrenaline like he hadn't felt in years.

He'd thought there was a burglar. When he first heard the sounds, he knew they didn't belong in the house where he'd lived his entire life. His brain had automatically drifted down dark alleys with nefarious characters. Not surprising for a horror fiction author.

Then again, he'd never experienced an intruder in this house. Just to be sure, he'd slowly made his way down the back stairs. Spying what he thought was a young man, he stalked him as he came into the center rotunda. A teenager, he'd thought. Maybe someone who'd been dared to sneak inside Sabatini House, the place of legends.

Instead, Tate found a woman pressed against him in his tight grip.

She came only to the hollow of his throat, even though she had to be taller than average. She froze in fear. Not that he blamed her. He'd be scared stiff, too, if he'd just broken into what he assumed to be an empty house.

Only this one was occupied.

He pressed his forearm down against her collarbone, careful to avoid the more fragile area of her neck. Though his knowledge of this hold was completely cerebral, he wanted to instill simple fear. Not find himself with a lawsuit on his hands.

"I asked you a question," he said, letting his voice drop even deeper. He carefully emphasized every word. "What are you doing in my house?"

"Your house?" she squeaked, trying to get her words out even though he could tell she was short of breath. From fear? *Good.* When she walked back out that door, he didn't want her or her friends to even think about coming back here.

"What are you talking about?" she gasped.

He loosened his hold, giving the impression of leniency even though he had no intention of giving in to whatever she wanted. But if he wanted answers, he needed her to talk. "How about *you* answer the questions?" he demanded. "Who are you?"

Her sudden lunge forward took him by surprise. He loosened his grip and let her go, not wanting to injure her just to keep her contained. After all, she couldn't escape. There wasn't a place in this house he couldn't find her.

But she went only as far as the stairs, sinking down to grab her flashlight. From her crouch against the railing she let the beam slowly travel up the length of him. "You can't be Mr. Kingston," she breathed as the light paused right below his face.

"Clearly I am."

"No…" That breathless quality distracted him more than he cared to admit. "Mr. Kingston is…um…"

"Is what?"

This time she didn't answer.

"Look, I don't care why you're here. But if you leave right now, I won't contact the police."

Behind her flashlight he could barely make out a frown.

"But I'm supposed to be here," she said.

What? "I don't think so."

"I am," she insisted, her voice quickly firming up. "I'm the new housekeeper."

For a moment Tate's very active brain froze. Somehow this scenario had never occurred to him. "Absolutely not."

Now it was her turn to ask. "Why?"

"You cannot be my new housekeeper."

Murdoch would not have done that to me.

Tate let his own powerful flashlight travel up her body, till the beam hit her full in the face. His author brain kicked in automatically, narrating the view. Pale, creamy skin. Hair that glinted fire, even in the strong light. And a thin, soaked T-shirt that outlined her curves perfectly beneath an open rain jacket.

She eased to her feet, blinking to adjust her sight. "I am the new housekeeper," she insisted. "Murdoch hired me."

"You can't be. The new housekeeper is a man. Will Harden."

She slapped her hand on her hip. "Uh, no. It's me. Willow Harden."

Damn Murdoch.

"I know I was supposed to be here earlier," she explained, "but things got pretty complicated with the storm moving in early. The power was out here and I worried, um, that you were okay."

"As you can see, I'm neither old nor in need of assistance." Yet. Though some days he felt every one of his thirty-eight years and more. He ignored the discomfort of that thought and continued, "I'm perfectly prepared for the weather. I certainly didn't need you to break into my house to check on me."

"I didn't break in. Murdoch gave me the keys."

Of course he did. "And the codes?"

"Yes, sir."

As her voice grew small, Tate recognized that the bully method of questioning wasn't helping anything.

Obviously he'd been fed incorrect information on purpose. Murdoch knew Tate would view a woman as a threat. An unwanted intrusion to a life spent making amends for his mistakes. Deadly mistakes.

Heck, that was probably why Murdoch had done it. He'd been different since finding his daughter again, since deciding to visit her for the first time. But that didn't mean Tate had to live with his friend's decisions.

This woman had to go.

They stood there in the dark, flashlights trained on each other like weapons. Tate would have found the situation amusing if he wasn't faced with the complications she represented. There was no way he could tolerate this intrusion.

"Well, I appreciate your concern, Ms. Harden—"

"Willow."

"—but I'm well equipped for this kind of thing. If you're a Savannah native, you know that the power goes out on these islands quite easily. I have lanterns, a portable cookstove, stored water, a generator—everything I need."

Her light dipped. Tate wondered what she was thinking. Why the hell would Murdoch hire a woman to come in and take care of Sabatini House while he visited his new grandchild? Granted, Tate hadn't specified gender when they'd discussed Murdoch's stand-in, but it should have been a given considering his history.

When she didn't speak further, he figured he needed

to spell it out. "Well, *Willow*, since I'm not what you wanted. And you aren't what I…"

He caught the lift of one eyebrow. Somehow he could read the warning for him to choose his words carefully. The fact that he understood that unspoken communication, and the earlier joy that had streaked through his body as he'd been pressed against her softness, convinced him she definitely had to go.

Joy was the last thing he deserved…and having her in this house would be nothing more than a temptation.

He continued carefully, "You aren't what *I expected*, so I think it would be best if we called this whole thing off. Don't you?"

He wasn't certain, but he thought she mumbled *Are you sure about that?* under her breath. The sound of the rain doubling down outside made it hard to tell.

"Obviously Murdoch made a mistake," he said.

"Nooo," she countered, shaking her head. "No, he didn't. He was very specific in his instructions. And after all this time, he knew I would follow them to the letter."

Tate tried to squelch his curiosity, but the words slipped out anyway. "How long have you known Murdoch?"

He could see her muscles loosen a little, softening her stance. "We met early last year. He's such a sweet man, once he lets you get to know him."

That's exactly how Tate would describe the man who'd been with him through the last twenty years of self-imposed exile from most of the world. Murdoch had been with him through the death of both his parents, the sale of his first book, but mostly he'd been there for Tate as he dealt with the grief that seemed never-ending. Murdoch had mentioned on more than one occasion that Tate's lifestyle wasn't healthy, but that simple opinion wouldn't change the choices Tate had made.

Couldn't change them.

Then Murdoch had said he was leaving…and now here Tate was facing the only woman to be in this house since his mother died.

"Look," she said, taking a step closer. "Murdoch would never forgive me if I walked away after all of the trouble he went through to make sure this place was taken care of while he was gone. Please. Just give me a chance."

Tate let his eyelids slide shut. The first thing that came to mind weren't words, as was often the case, but the memory of her body against his. The close heat. The sweet scent. The softness of curves.

Nope. Bad idea. He crossed his arms over his chest, knowing full well his bulk could be intimidating.

Probably reading the rejection in his stance, Willow continued, "Besides, how will you hire someone else? Phone calls. Interviews. How many will it take before you find the right person?"

"No."

No more intrusion. Anger rose as Tate tried to think, quickly. This woman was way too smart, and well-armed with info. Uneasiness slithered through him as he wondered what else Murdoch might have told her.

But the aggression in his tone didn't seem to faze her. "Or you could just accept the inevitable," she continued.

"And that is?"

"Without me, you're gonna have a ton of people tromping all through this place. From what Murdoch said, that's not something you would enjoy."

"Or I could settle for just you?"

He caught her sneaky smile on the outer edge of his flashlight glow. Then she asked, "Besides, have you driven in this stuff recently?" She flicked the flashlight toward one of the massive windows behind him. "I thought I was going to die trying to get here. I have no desire to go back out into this weather."

"A little melodramatic, aren't you?" Even he cringed at his condescending tone. Defensiveness didn't sit well on him.

But on her... The way she stiffened her spine put other attributes on display. Tate tried not to notice.

"Are you kidding me?" she demanded. "You obviously haven't tried driving a tiny car over that bridge in fifty-mile-an-hour wind gusts. Have you?"

Tate felt himself automatically shut down. No, he hadn't driven in this kind of weather...not for many, many years. And he never would. Certainly not over the narrow bridge that connected the island to the mainland.

"I made a lot of effort to get here. It's at least common courtesy to let me try to do the job."

Tate clenched his jaw, frustration tightening his tone. "If you stay, you won't find courtesy to be one of my strong points."

This time she didn't respond, but adopted a stance that mimicked his own. In that moment, Tate recognized her.

Oh, he'd never met her before, but he'd described her type over and over in his work. She was the embodiment of the heroines he wrote about in his horror stories. Women with grit, determination and smarts who made it out alive when lesser mortals rarely survived.

That tingling awareness he'd been doing his best to ignore multiplied. All the more reason to get her out of here.

A flash of white lit the room as lightning suddenly streaked across the night sky. Tate saw her jaw clench and shoulders straighten as she braced herself. Admirable. It was a little clue that told him a lot about her. Heck, the fact that she'd made it here in the first place in this weather signified a strength and determination some people never displayed in their lifetime.

The flash was followed closely by a hard clap of thunder. The storm was picking up again. But it was just starting for Tate.

Somehow he knew giving in on this point meant he would lose this battle...and lose the war. But she was right. As a long roll of thunder shook the house, he knew he couldn't send her back out in this weather. His own feelings about her presence aside, he refused to make an impulsive decision that cost someone their life.

Again.

"Let me show you to a room, then."

Two

At least he had let her stay instead of forcing her back out into the weather.

The consolation was mild as her overactive brain was assaulted with emotions. First the drive and the storm, then the dark house, and now being led up this magnificent staircase by a tall, brooding man carrying an old-fashioned lantern. If she wanted atmosphere, she'd received it in abundance.

Actually, more than she'd hoped for.

She shivered, though she couldn't tell if it was because of her still-damp shirt or the continued uncertainty of this entire situation.

Tate led her only a short way down the hall before pausing beside a closed door. As with the ones she'd seen downstairs, there were intricate carvings, swirls and maybe leaves and vines that gave the wood dimension. Even in the gloom it was gorgeous. "This will be your room for the night."

So, he still wouldn't concede that she was right?

"Where's yours?" she asked, only to clamp her lips together in regret.

In the light of the lantern she watched one thick, dark brow rise. "I'm in a suite at the end of the hall," he answered simply.

Right.

The darkened room beyond slowly came to life as Tate lit candles from a fireplace match. Willow stared in awe as the historical setting came to life. A large silver candelabrum on the dresser provided most of the light, with smaller candlesticks dotted around the room. As Tate's big body moved through the shadows, fear and fascination mingled inside of her.

A four-poster bed with drapes and some kind of fabric topper dominated the space, the white fabric with navy filigree pattern lending to the old-fashioned feel of the room. Add in the tall man with shoulder-length disheveled hair and she had the makings of a regular *Wuthering Heights* on her hands. The thought sent another shiver over her.

As he turned to look at her, she became all too conscious of her body's reaction. She'd love to blame it on the cold, but she feared the tightening of her nipples had more to do with the man standing before her than the temperature. She quickly crossed her arms over her chest.

Let him make of that what he wanted.

"It's beautiful," she murmured. Even in the shadows, there was no mistaking the intricate designs on the furniture and fabrics.

His gruff command grated on her nerves. "Don't get too attached. We will discuss this situation in the morning."

"Really? We're still not over that, are we?" She wasn't sure what gave her the gumption to say it, but as she stood there shivering with cold, she was over his attitude.

He raised those dark brows again. "I may require more patience than you possess."

There was almost a literary quality to his pronunciation that sharpened the edge of his words.

Maybe he was right, but… "I have more patience than you could imagine. After all, I teach history to eighteen-year-old freshmen who think being at college gives them the freedom to do whatever they want."

Her response seemed to surprise him, lightening his expression a little. "The fearlessness to enter a dark house, the patience of a saint… Is there anything else Murdoch didn't tell me about you?"

I'm attracted to tall, dark and mysterious men? "Um…a classroom of eighty of those monsters has made me efficient, organized and slightly entertaining?"

"Do you really call them monsters?"

This time she didn't hold back a cheeky grin. "To their faces—with the utmost of affection, I assure you."

"Then I can only imagine what you'd call me."

Before she could come up with a clever response, he was at the door. "Good night," he said as he left the room, closing the door behind him.

At least he didn't lock me in.

Willow half grinned, half whimpered at the thought. Her sisters would take away her modern-woman card if they knew she'd been seriously attracted to the dark brooding man in the darkened house on the isolated island. Somehow she'd been cast in her very own Gothic mystery with a leading man who would fit right in with Hollywood's most gorgeous heartthrobs.

But she had a feeling he saw her more as a nuisance than a leading lady. She'd do well to remember that.

Despite wanting to get out of her damp clothes and shoes, Willow took a moment to slowly turn around in the middle of the room. This place was incredible. The furniture she'd seen in the other rooms had been antique, too, but this was an incredibly high-quality fairy-tale look that she'd seen only in photographs.

The bedroom was fit for a royal prince, even if Murdoch had only been the hired help. Willow jumped as lightning flashed through the sheer window coverings, then giggled as she glanced around. The dark furniture was offset by the creamy color of the bed draperies that almost matched the ivory walls. There was a heavy chifforobe, a dresser with an oval mirror hanging above it that reflected the light from the large silver candelabra and matching bedside tables. A large navy carpet mimicked the pattern of the drapes. It looked so soft, Willow couldn't wait to dig in her cold toes.

Conscious of how damp she was, she glanced in the chifforobe for anything to cover herself with, but it was empty. Well, she wasn't going back out in this weather for her suitcase, and Tate hadn't offered. She would just have to make do.

At least her current dilemma took her mind off the man sleeping in the suite at the end of the hall.

She flipped the cream-colored duvet down to the end of the bed, grateful to find another blanket beneath it. As she removed her jeans and wet shoes, she tried to think of ways she could convince Tate to let her stay. This was a short-term gig. Murdoch had chosen her personally. She could prove she was good at the job... if Tate would just give her the chance to show him.

She blew out all the candles except a couple right beside her bed. The urge to search out the dark corners of the room still irked her. But even crawling under the warm blanket didn't relax her. Exhaustion lurked just below the surface, but her overactive brain wouldn't let it take over.

Maybe she could make him her special French toast for breakfast? They said food was the way to a man's heart. Maybe showcasing her cooking skills would at least soften his.

As she reached for her phone to set an alarm, a noise caught her attention. The deep creak of old wood sounded above her, reminding her of her mission and renewing her courage. She needed this job. She needed to find out the secrets her great-grandmother had hinted at in her journals.

Just remember that, little miss!

More creaking, then a thud overhead had Willow sitting up. That sounded like more than just an old house settling in. Had Tate gone upstairs before going to bed? She hadn't heard any footsteps, but—

Bam!

Willow tucked herself down in the bed, instincts insisting those few inches would save her. But when nothing else happened, she giggled a little. Boy, tonight's atmospheric adventures were sure affecting her.

Drip. Drip.

Willow bent over to inspect the water droplet that had landed on her now-bare calf. Where was that coming from? She glanced up at the material above her. The heavy drapes were gathered in the middle, creating myriad folds that revealed nothing. The lack of light wasn't helping. Curiosity getting the better of her, she lifted up onto her knees for a better vantage point. That might be water droplets hanging from the fabric. Maybe?

Then the world went dark as the creak became a crash.

Tate debated whether to go back to work or give it up for the night. He'd been moving along at a fast clip when he'd heard Willow downstairs. But the conflicting emotions of the last hour had left him growlier than a grizzly bear. He usually didn't write well in that state. Working out would be better, but with the electricity off he'd better not be wandering around in the basement.

Also he probably needed to keep an ear peeled for his houseguest for a little while. Something told him she needed supervision. A feeling that had nothing to do with wanting to get his hands on her again. *Absolutely nothing.*

Suddenly he could feel the approaching crash on the final lap of his adrenaline rush. Yeah, writing would be impossible in a matter of minutes. His brain would fog over and the words simply wouldn't be able to break through. Better to rest now and write tomorrow—after he'd dealt with the problem lurking in Murdoch's bedroom in the form of one sexy redhead.

Tate strolled into the office to shut off the battery-operated lantern he'd left in there earlier. Before he cut off the light, he paused, staring at the shutters closed tightly over the windows. Heavy rain beat against the house, but here the sound was muffled. The last thing Tate had wanted to see was the choppy waves of the sea below, stirred up by the storm.

Haunting memories rose despite his mental protest. Maybe he wouldn't be able to sleep tonight, after all.

As he flipped the switch on the lantern, another noise joined the rest. It was so faint he almost missed it. Moving back toward the hall, he wondered if his guest had come to find him. He hoped not. He had willpower like a suit of armor, but she seemed to be able to find every weak point.

Then he heard the booming crash. He hurried down the empty hall until he reached her room. A commotion was in progress behind the door. What the hell?

He swung the door open, then froze. The door slammed against the wall. Before him…he wasn't even sure what was happening. A writhing mass of wet bedclothes, splintered pieces of wood and dripping water occupied the bed…instead of the slightly damp housekeeper he'd left here thirty minutes before.

For a moment, the scene captured his artistic imagination. Despite the urge to rush in, he had to catalog it for future reference. And frankly, he was enjoying the show.

The frantic wiggling granted him glimpses of nicely rounded calves. He should help untangle her, he really should. Then she froze. He could just hear the quick intake of breath before she screamed, "Help me!"

That galvanized him into action. He struggled to find an opening as she thrashed about. "Be still," he snapped.

His low command seemed to make it through to her because she paused long enough for him to snag the edge of the fabric. With a heavy tug, he divested her of the soggy bed curtains.

Then had the immediate urge to cover her back up.

As her bare calves had warned him, she'd taken off her jeans. And her bra. She now crouched, breathing hard, in the middle of the bed wearing nothing but a wet T-shirt and panties. Her wild auburn hair flew in every direction, including over her lightly freckled face. If he'd had twinges of attraction earlier, they were nothing compared with now.

Finally she reached up and tossed her hair back from her face. Tate quickly directed his gaze up to the ceiling. Whoa. Leaning over, he got a better angle to see what had happened. The substantial hole over her bed revealed only the darkened room above and the steady drip of water that he suspected came from dislodged tiles on the roof.

Straightening, he then let his gaze track back to the woman in the middle of the mess. "Don't guess you will be sleeping here tonight. There must be some damage to the roof. In this part of the house, there's only the one floor above you. It was fine during the last inspection, but something might have hit it or the wind must have ripped something loose."

Reaching out, he plucked her from the bed. Her squeal echoed around the room. The distinctly feminine sound jump-started his heart. He hadn't heard someone make a sound like that since he was a teenager. The women he met now didn't squeal. They wouldn't consider it sexy.

"Let's get you settled somewhere else," he said.

She was already shaking her head, sending her hair flying once more. "We need to clean up first," she insisted. To his surprise she started gathering the mess into the middle of the bed.

While the thought was appreciated, her movements afforded Tate an even better view. The T-shirt barely covered her upper thighs. The expanse of smooth skin was mouthwatering. "I'll get something to catch the water," he murmured.

Escape was a relief, but a brief one.

When he returned with a large plastic tub, he found himself eye level with a pair of silky panties he'd have been better off not seeing. "What are you doing?" he growled.

Willow jerked, her shock unbalancing her and the candle in her hand as she stood on the bed.

"Woman," he snapped. "Let's not catch the bed on fire, too."

She frowned at him. "This isn't my fault. I was just trying to see what had caused the leak."

"I'll investigate in the morning." He glanced over the now-stripped bed and soggy mattress. "And get this all replaced."

There was no helping it. His gaze snagged on creamy white thighs below the edge of her T-shirt. She might not have realized how she looked before, but now was different. Her delicate hand came into view, tugging the hem down. He flicked his gaze up to her face, only to see a red stain spreading across her skin. Yep, she was fully aware now.

"Let me help you," he murmured, then had to clear his throat as his voice deepened without his permission.

Still she accepted his hand for balance as she climbed down. The shocking chill of her skin as it met his made him shift gears from lust to more practical matters. Like where she was going to sleep...

He placed the tub carefully in the middle of the bed to catch the dripping water. Good thing it wasn't coming down heavier. "This should halt the damage for a while. It should stop raining in a couple of hours," he said.

Willow offered a brief nod, then skirted around behind him. "I've got to see about some clothes," she said, her voice sounding strangled.

He shouldn't have made her uncomfortable, but the rest of the night would make matters much worse.

"Where do you think you're going?" he asked as she scooted toward the open doorway.

"I guess I'll have to go out to the car to get my bags." She paused, then inched back inside. "I should probably put on some shoes for that."

"You aren't going out in this weather." As if to back him up, lightning flashed outside, then thunder rumbled loud enough to rattle the windows. "We will find something else for you." He gestured for her to go out into the hall, but she hesitated.

Tate had a feeling this was where living as a single man and not as part of a family was going to bite him in the ass. He turned smartly on his heel and headed back the way he'd come, silently gesturing for her to follow. He ignored her questions, trying to get everything straight in his own mind first. With a sense of trepidation that he kept well hidden, he walked straight into his bedroom and opened the top drawer of the bureau, pulling out a well-worn T-shirt. He turned back to see her hovering in the doorway.

"You might as well come inside," he snapped.

"Why?"

Her obvious hesitation reminded him that the situation wasn't her fault and was completely out of both of their control. He tempered his tone.

"Because this is where the only other bed in the house is," he said with a voice full of resignation.

She stepped through the doorway, her eyes wide with shock. "What?"

He spoke a little more slowly. "This is the only bed… And the only decent sofa is right there." He pointed back toward the living area that comprised half the large master suite. "We're going to share a room tonight, I'm afraid."

Even in the dim light he could see her eyes cataloging everything she'd seen tonight—which wasn't much. Still, she tried. "But there are so many rooms—"

"Which have been stripped. Or I assure you the mattresses are nothing but dust and springs by now."

He held out the oversize T. "Your attire, my dear."

Three

Even with the sound of heavy rain outside, Willow could still hear every squeak of the leather when Tate moved on the couch. And he moved a lot.

Too bad it wasn't thundering still.

As the furniture protested yet another turn of Tate's big body, Willow contemplated their current situation in the dark. She knew Murdoch had said they never had visitors, but she never imagined a big house like this wouldn't at least be set up for the possibility. This was the South. Hospitality was an actual way of life down here. All these rooms lying dormant would be unheard of.

It was a type of isolation Willow couldn't imagine. She should be sound asleep right now. Between the tense drive and the stress of meeting her new boss, exhaustion weighed down her bones. But her unexpected dousing in cold water and ceiling tiles had her hyped. And every squeak of the leather told her Tate was in the same boat.

As one particularly restless move was followed by a long sigh, Willow finally gave in. She sat up and projected her voice above the noise of raindrops hitting the windows. "This is ridiculous. Come to bed."

Hmm…that probably wasn't the right way to put it. Now that her vision had adjusted somewhat to the dark, she could see his head and bare shoulders rise above the back of the couch. "What did you say?"

She should have been intimidated, but she was over that by now. "Come sleep in your own bed. You're never gonna get any rest over there. And neither am I."

"What's that supposed to mean?"

"That every time you move that couch creaks. It's even noisier than the rain outside."

He slowly got to his feet. To her relief, he wrapped a blanket around his shoulders, covering the light skin that she wanted so badly to see. To cover her awkwardness over having her gorgeous new boss approach the bed she was sleeping in, she said the first thing that came to mind.

"At least the one good bed left in the house is the size of a football field." Frankly, she felt a little lost in all this yardage.

"I'm not a small guy."

To that, she could attest.

"But I don't think this is a good idea," he said.

"*I think* we'll manage," she said, her sense of humor asserting itself. "I won't think less of you if you put pillows down the middle. After all, I want you to feel safe."

Even in the dark she caught his pause. "Shouldn't that be my line?" he asked. She detected a touch of amusement. Probably the best she could hope for with him, especially since his progress had slowed considerably. Did walking toward her on the bed have to resemble a death march?

Not that he should be too eager, but still...

"I'm not the one who needs convincing," she reminded him. "And if I don't get some sleep soon, I'll have trouble proving my worth to my new boss tomorrow."

This time she was granted a chuckle, and he finished making his way across the room. The bed shifted a little as he lay down, but he seemed to stay as close to the edge as possible. Heck, her arm fully stretched out wouldn't come close to reaching him.

"No pillows?" she finally asked.

"I think I'm safe."

You wish. She tried to relax, tried to sink into the most comfortable mattress she'd ever lain on, but it wasn't happening. Then he suddenly spoke.

"Considering how well you've taken everything that's happened tonight, I think you might have earned a point or two in your favor. Hopefully your new boss will agree."

She huffed out a little laugh, then consciously forced her muscles to clench, then relax. It was the only thing she knew of to distract herself from his presence. So close, but still a good distance away.

That's the way she should want it, but a niggling desire wouldn't be smothered. If what he'd said was true, she'd have to learn to live with lusting after her boss in the quiet recesses of her own mind.

Though she'd thought sleep wouldn't show up, considering the thoughts running rampant through her brain, the steady sound of the rain, the exhaustion she couldn't fight any longer and the even breath of the man a few feet away eventually lured her under.

She woke to a different environment altogether. Instead of rain, sunshine peeked through the slats that protected the windows. Heavy covers kept her warm. Her body, her muscles, felt languid, almost liquefied in her relaxation. Then something shifted against her leg and sleep was immediately a thing of the past.

Suddenly the weight against her back and lower body made more sense. It wasn't a heavy blanket. It was a man.

Her heart picked up speed. She lay on her stomach. His chest seemed to be covering part of her back. Now that she knew what to look for, she could see his fingers against the covers on the opposite side of her body. His warm, musky scent clung to the sheets, tempting her to draw in a deep breath.

But would even that slight movement wake him up?

As incredibly sexy as this was, and as much as her body throbbed its approval, the last thing she wanted was to face him knowing his leg had slid between hers. Why hadn't he stayed on his side of the football field?

He shifted, rubbing a warm, hairy leg against the sensitive skin of her inner thighs. The shirt he'd given her hung almost to her knees, but now she had a feeling her panties were exposed…and probably a little damp.

She needed out now. But how did she do that?

Above her hair, she heard a heavy sigh. The big body half covering hers stretched, pressing harder against her. A certain part of him was making its approval well-known. Willow bit her lip to keep a groan inside. Why did he have to feel so good?

Then he went absolutely still.

She squeezed her eyes shut. *I don't want to deal with this.* And she certainly didn't want him to see how much she enjoyed waking up to his body pressed against hers. But as he shifted infinitesimally, she braced herself for the inevitable awkward confrontation.

"Oh no," he groaned softly behind her.

Oh yes. The only thing to do was guard her expression as best as possible and brave this out. Twisting around, she tried to blink innocently. "Sleep well?"

"Not my usual," he said, his voice deep and gravelly enough to send tingles along her nerve endings.

She tried to ignore his heavy eyelids, sleepy expression and tousled black hair. But this whole "barely awake" look was short-circuiting her overloaded brain. "Pardon me?"

"Sleeping is usually a solitary experience."

Even though the past twelve hours had proved that guests weren't an option around here, she had a difficult time believing this hot, virile male only slept alone. "Seriously?"

Pulling away, he sat up on the edge of the bed. With him facing away from her, she couldn't read his expression. She had a feeling that was on purpose.

His voice was low when he spoke, though not as gravelly as earlier. "I haven't slept in the same room with another person since I was a teenager."

As he walked away, Willow marveled for a moment. Considering how good it had felt to lie with him in this bed, she'd have thought he'd had plenty of experience in this area.

Or any area related to the bedroom.

Tate was glad Willow had disappeared by the time he came out of his dressing room. The tremor in his hands as he'd washed up and dressed had startled him.

The desire had hit him hard and fast.

Not since he'd been an untried youth had he been near a woman he had to have. His casual liaisons focused more on one-night stands to scratch an itch. He could appreciate a beautiful woman, even desire one. But urgency was definitely a thing of the past for him.

Yet his body's response to Willow had been all-consuming. If it hadn't been awkward enough to curb him, they would still be in his big bed—a whole lot more naked than they'd been upon awakening.

He breathed through the sudden surge of his body, waiting until his response died down before making his way out the door and downstairs. Instead of the sound of crashing thunder, the rooms now echoed with the rumble of waves beneath the house. The sound was muted as he moved down the hall to the kitchen.

There he found Willow bent over, inspecting the contents of the fridge. His body pulsed, responding to the sight of feminine curves encased in still-damp jeans.

His body was happy. His brain was not. This response was downright unsettling.

"What are you doing?" he asked, a little too gruff.

He felt bad about his tone when she jumped, bumping her ginger head into the lower edge of the freezer door. Her low moan made it worse, because it brought to mind things he shouldn't be thinking about around her. He'd never had sex with anyone in Sabatini House since he'd become an adult. He hadn't been lying when he'd told her that he hadn't slept with anyone. Though why those words had come out in that moment, he had no idea.

Just say what you need to say and get out of here.

But words escaped him as she turned to face him.

Seeing her in full sunlight was like living color compared with the black-and-white of last night. Willow had the classic pale skin of a redhead with just a fine dusting of freckles across her cheeks. She had emerald-green eyes, which was what he favored for the female characters he wrote about, but in person hers were so vibrant. She was tall for a woman, just as he'd noticed last night, but now he could see all the sexy curves he hadn't had a chance to truly savor this morning.

He cleared his throat, glancing out the window behind her to steady himself. Which wasn't as effective as looking seaside. That would have reminded him of exactly why this woman was off-limits to a man like him. But at least the view of the barren hill leading to the gates below calmed the resurgence of desire that thrummed through his veins.

As if his silence was an invitation, Willow jumped right in. "I'm just checking to see what the inventory is like." Crossing to the island, she picked up a pen and tapped it against the pad of paper lying there. "The landline is still out, but when we can get through, here are some places I'll call about the roof and repairs—with your permission, of course."

Though he'd prefer to direct this discussion himself, focusing on action was a very good idea right now. "Why wait? I'll get the satellite phone from my office."

She raised a brow. "Murdoch didn't mention that you had a satellite phone."

"I prefer to forget I have it. My editor, Charles, insisted I get it because he got tired of my being out of reach and ignoring his emails. The landline goes down all the time out here. I only use it to call him and my agent and for emergencies."

He could tell by her face that this little explanation puzzled her, but Tate wasn't going out of his way to explain his eccentricities. That was the way he operated. She could take it or leave it.

He glanced over the list. "These two," he said, pointing to a couple of companies he'd worked with in the past. She had good taste. "I'll get your luggage while you put in the calls."

"What? So you were serious—"

"If you haven't slapped me yet, I guess we're pretty close to compatible. And it saves me the time of searching for a housekeeper to hold me over for just two months."

Willow started a little happy dance on her side of the island. Tate did his best to ignore the sway of soft body parts.

This decision was probably a mistake, but it was expedient. And after accosting her in his sleep he felt obligated to be rather generous.

"So let me know when they arrive, and I'll show them around."

"I can handle it," she quickly countered.

Tate adopted his sternest expression. "But I know the house, so I will. Got it?"

"Yeeesss…" The drawn-out word made it clear she didn't understand, but she would soon enough.

"I'll give you a chance to clean up, then we'll go over a few things," he said, eager for a break from his unrelenting response to her presence.

"We can now," she said, eagerness practically vibrating off her in waves. "I'm good."

Maybe getting it over with was a good choice. Like ripping a bandage off a particularly sensitive patch of skin.

"Let's start with the rules."

She blinked, as if trying to comprehend what he was saying.

"What did Murdoch tell you?"

Her smile opened her face up, revealing a pleasure that sunk straight into Tate's darkened heart. He couldn't catch his breath for a moment. Luckily she didn't notice as she bent over to pull a notebook from her backpack. Guess she wasn't a designer purse kind of girl.

"He gave me a whole notebook on house procedures. Let's see, gate and alarm codes, chore schedule, your favorite foods…"

But no real rules? Somehow at this point he wasn't surprised. Yesterday he would have been. Not today.

But Tate was a big believer in start how you mean to go on…

"Rule number one. I am not to be disturbed."

That seemed pretty self-explanatory, but Willow still asked, "You mean when you're writing?"

Tate refused to show the jolt of surprise that shot through him. "So Murdoch told you what I do for a living?"

"Actually, the fact that you're an author is pretty well-known and speculated on in Savannah. Though no one has been able to crack the answer to what you actually write."

"And Murdoch didn't share that."

The solemn shake of her head didn't dampen the curiosity in her expression. But he wasn't about to satisfy her with an answer. Instead he ignored the whole line of questioning.

"Actually, when I'm in my office at all, I'm not to be disturbed. I'll come down at the set mealtimes I'm sure Murdoch gave you."

Willow quickly moved on. "What about mail? Do you want your mail when it comes, or for me to wait for a meal and give it to you then?"

As she opened her mouth to say something else, Tate raised his hand for her to stop. "Do. Not. Disturb. Understand?"

He could see another question brewing in those green eyes, but he forged ahead. "Rule number two. No talking about me or anything that happens here or that you see here outside of these premises."

"What about with my family?"

That wasn't an issue Tate had ever run into with

Murdoch. He and his family had been estranged for the first ten years he had worked here, but even after the reconciliation Murdoch hadn't shared important details of his job with them. He'd simply gotten into the habit of keeping Tate's issues private.

But Willow's family might be a different story.

"I think that rule is self-explanatory," he said, injecting a stern note into his tone.

"Actually, it's not," Willow said. "I mean, I'm guessing you want me to keep quiet about who you are, since Murdoch did. What about the house? Can I talk about it? Am I supposed to keep quiet about everything I see? Where's the line? Can I tell my family how to contact me?"

"Of course."

She'd asked more than one question, and the litany confused him. Murdoch was a quiet, loner type. Willow was not quiet…at all.

"Of course you can tell your family the landline number, as long as they don't abuse it or share it," he amended. "But my home, my business, are to be kept private at all times."

"Do I need to sign a nondisclosure agreement?"

"I don't know. Do you?"

The rapid shake of her head sent wisps of red hair flying. Man, that was gorgeous. This woman was all living color. He looked back out the windows.

"Certain rooms in the house are off-limits to everyone but me."

"Murdoch mentioned that, but how will I know which ones they are?"

"Good God, woman, do you ever stop asking questions?"

Tate looked back at her just in time to see her blink hard. For a moment, he feared he might be facing tears, but no. Just a sad "Sorry. I guess I just want to do it right the first time."

Man, I'm such a jerk.

Tate's brain scrambled to rectify the situation. He heard himself say, "I'll take you around and show you." Until now, he'd had no intention of doing any such thing.

And the way her eyes lit up made him think what should be a simple thirty-minute walk would turn into hours of her asking questions he didn't want to answer. "Later," he added.

He might need to fortify himself with a drink…or two…beforehand.

Four

Willow wasn't stupid.

She knew her curiosity tended to get on people's nerves. A lifelong learner—that's what one of her professors in college had called her. The insatiable curiosity and hunger for knowledge made her annoying to some people and boring to most.

Her sisters loved pretty dresses, nail polish and all things feminine. And while Willow had a good enough eye to help them pick things out, she had no desire for those things herself. Instead she was excited by books, old houses and antiques. If there was a mystery to go along with them, all the better.

She seemed to get on Tate's nerves more than most. Which was too bad. Because he was a hunk.

All those glorious muscles, that messy hair and brooding intense stare. He matched the mysterious house to perfection... But he wasn't well matched with her. She could tell he'd enjoyed her much more in his sleep—when she wasn't talking.

After a morning spent inspecting the kitchen and fixing his lunch, she waited impatiently for him to finish eating. He took his time in the breakfast nook, while she struggled not to eagerly bounce from foot to foot in the kitchen. She'd snuck a peek at some of the adjacent rooms, but she was eager to see the rest of the house... even if it was just a tour for him to show her what she wasn't allowed to touch.

Finally he brought his plate back into the kitchen.

"Is it time now?" she asked, then pressed her lips together, inwardly chastising herself for her impatience.

He raised one dark brow, but this time seemed rather amused by her enthusiasm instead of annoyed.

He gestured toward the hallway leading to the rotunda. "Shall we?"

As they walked down the hall, she once more glanced into the open rooms. For the most part, they were bare. Some were decorated with boxes and sheet-covered lumps that could have been furniture. Intricately carved doors and elaborate lighting fixtures coated in dust reinforced their lack of use.

As they reached the rotunda, Tate paused. He braced himself in the middle of the round room, staring up the magnificent staircase as if he were challenging it. A multitiered chandelier that Willow hadn't been able to make out in the dark hung from the very high ceiling. A row of small windows around the top of the rotunda let in light that bounced off the chandelier's crystals.

"Sabatini House was built by a pirate," he started, his voice echoing slightly off the walls. "It took over ten years to complete, though he brought his bride here after only three. It's built to celebrate the spot where the water forges its connection with the land."

Willow started to open her mouth, started to question whether the stories of the underground caves were true, but then she remembered the cut of his reprimand this morning. She quickly closed it again.

The last thing she needed was to aggravate Tate at the moment. She'd hold all of her questions as long as she possibly could. After all, she wanted him to be able to at least tolerate her. Maybe there would be a time to ask her questions later, after he got used to her being around.

Or maybe she could settle for something benign? Like "How long have you lived here?"

"The house has had a long and varied history," Tate said. "My family were direct descendants, so I've lived here all of my life."

She thought of how much her own little house meant to her and her family. It wasn't anything as magnificent as this, but it was a direct link to their people. "Wow," she said. "That must be an incredible feeling."

The indistinct noise Tate made drew her gaze away

from the impressive rotunda to his face. He stared at nothing with a deep frown. "Both a blessing and a curse," he said.

She ached for him to explain, but he simply turned away. Where was his family now? she wondered. Why did they leave him all alone? These were definitely questions she should *not* ask.

And he certainly wasn't volunteering that information.

Instead he kept to the general. "The house was built to withstand the rough weather of the outer islands. Tropical storms, hurricanes, flooding—they all pose a threat. But not to Sabatini House. After a lifetime living on ships at sea, that pirate knew exactly what he was up against. Even the erosion of the ocean was guarded against when building the foundation."

Curiosity burned in Willow's throat. He had to be referring to the flood of the ocean beneath the mansion. Were the rumors true? Murdoch had refused to deny or confirm the existence of caves beneath Sabatini House, stating it wasn't his place to say.

Tate's strong legs carried him up the stairs. "Sabatini House doesn't have an elevator. All the upper floors are reached through this staircase, or the one on the opposite end from the kitchen. If a room is locked, it is off-limits to you. That includes the third floor."

Panic swallowed up Willow's reserve. "But what if—"

Tate paused, twisting around to stare down at her from a few steps above. "Off. Limits."

"Right," she mumbled as they continued up the stairs. She struggled not to show her unease. Her personal reasons for taking this job included finding the answer to a family mystery…an answer that probably hid in one of the third-floor rooms, if Murdoch's information was correct.

Resolving to find a way, Willow focused once more on the current tour.

As they traversed several hallways, Tate gave short explanations about architecture, molding and carvings in the plaster. But nothing personal. Nothing meaningful. He could have been a boring docent in a beautiful museum for all the enthusiasm he infused in his words.

Many of the rooms were dusty. Some were completely empty. He hadn't been kidding when he said there wasn't another mattress in the place. One of the downstairs living areas had been decorated with "more modern" furniture from the fifties or sixties. Any bedrooms had empty bed frames—beautiful, but achingly empty. While Tate obviously understood the history of the house—the why and how it was built—that didn't translate into pride of ownership.

Willow's hands itched to work on some of the antiques that they passed. A large grandfather clock. Leather-bound books. Incredible pieces of furniture covered in dust cloths…or simply dust. Restoring antiques was a passionate hobby of hers, but she doubted Tate would appreciate her efforts.

They came to the wing on the second floor that Willow remembered from this morning. It was closed off from the main hall with heavy wooden doors carved with intricate swirled designs.

Tate paused. "This wing holds my suite of rooms," he said. "If these doors are open, you may come down the hall. You'll of course need to clean and gather laundry. But my office is absolutely off-limits."

He pulled the heavy floor-to-ceiling doors open with a loud creak. Guess there was no sneaking in here... She smothered a giggle. Tate didn't seem the type to appreciate her subversive brand of humor.

This hallway was darker than the others. Most of the adjoining doors were closed, cutting off the light from outside. Tate pointed to the far end. His face was grim as he said, "My bedroom suite. You can go in there to change the sheets or clean the bathroom. But cleaning only."

He pointed to a long table on one side of the hallway. "That door there is my office. If any mail comes that needs to be attended to, you can set it on the table and I'll get it when I'm ready."

He turned to study her, his expression almost expectant. She knew he was wondering why she didn't ask any questions. Her earlier behavior had proved her curiosity. But the questions she wanted to ask weren't appropriate. Like, why are you keeping these rooms off-limits? What is it you have to hide? Why can't I bring the mail to you, instead of just leaving it on the table outside?

None of his secrecy or demands for privacy made any sense.

Finally he continued, "The third story and turrets are off-limits."

It was a struggle not to roll her eyes like a smart-alecky teenager, despite the unease that resurfaced. She was beginning to think the word *off-limits* was his absolute favorite.

"There's nothing up there that you need to be involved in, and some of the rooms could be dangerous from disrepair. As evidenced by the roof caving in last night."

"I thought you said the roof had been inspected?"

"It is, yearly. But as you can see, in a house this old, anything is possible. Even when you're careful."

She trailed behind him as they went back down the stairs, only this time he curved around behind the staircase and down another, much smaller set of stairs. Her heart started to thud as the sound of the ocean grew louder in her ears.

"Down here you'll find the laundry room, and some storage areas where we keep extra supplies."

He walked down the hallway. The floor seemed to be carved straight out of rock. The laundry room was industrial-sized, but obviously converted from something else that had been there for many, many years. The storage room was lined with shelves. The cool atmosphere was perfect for storing a variety of items and keeping them fresh. She could just look around these rooms and see the history of them, feel how integral they had been to a huge busy household that had many mouths to feed. The history buff in her shivered with excitement.

The other side of the hall had one large, long room with a door open at each end. The space was full of exercise equipment. Guess she now knew where Tate's bulk came from.

"I work out every night." Gesturing toward a phone at one end of the room, he added, "You can reach me on the intercom here if necessary."

At least he wasn't *off-limits* when he was working out. Although seeing him half-dressed and sweaty might be more than she could resist. After all, that might make her forget his current attitude...

They made their way back toward the bottom of the staircase. Willow kept expecting him to mention the sound of the ocean and the underground cave that was rumored to be part of the house, but he never did. She'd been a good girl, keeping herself focused on the essentials and not plying him with questions. But as he took that first step up the stairs, she couldn't hold it in any longer.

"Is it true?"

He turned to stare down at her, his brooding look almost daring her to ask the question. But she couldn't help herself.

"Are there underground caves here beneath Sabatini House?"

His stare turned into a glare, and for long moments she thought he wouldn't answer. Then he came back down the steps to stand uncomfortably close. He pointed down the opposite hallway.

"Yes, it is true," he said, his voice low and rumbly. She could almost feel the vibration in her core. "The caves are actually natural, with parts that are hand-carved beneath the house's foundation. But they are completely—"

"Off-limits?" she supplied.

It was all she could do not to giggle when he glared down at her. "The swimming cove is not safe," he insisted. "Don't ever go in there."

"Why? How is it not safe?"

If nothing else, she just wanted a peek.

The question changed his tone from stern to downright cold. "I don't need a reason. Just stay away."

She shivered at his intensity. But that didn't kill her curiosity. As he turned to leave, she couldn't help but stare at the hall leading to the most mysterious part of the house.

What was it he was hiding?

If Willow had any doubts about Tate's determination that she stay away from the third floor, they disappeared when the repairmen arrived that afternoon.

She didn't even have to call him down—he simply appeared in the doorway to the kitchen as she watched the repair truck drive up the winding road and around to the side of the house. Tate had used this company before, so they knew where to enter.

Tate completely bypassed her, focusing all of his attention on Mr. Hobbins, the company's owner. Only the best for Sabatini House. Despite the need to help rising up in her, watching both the men was amusing in its own way.

Mr. Hobbins was obviously used to dealing with Murdoch. He glanced back and forth between Tate and her with a bemused expression, then looked behind Tate for good measure, as though Murdoch might be hiding there. He quickly recovered and offered Tate a "Good afternoon."

For his part, Tate exuded control and authority. But he didn't indulge in small talk. In fact, he didn't reach out to shake the man's hand, either. He launched into an explanation of the current issues that needed addressing. Mr. Hobbins's expression quickly transformed from polite to all business. They discussed what would need to be done, and Tate waved away the offer of an estimate. "Just do it right, whatever that costs. And quickly. We've got some more rain coming in later this week. We don't need new damage."

They walked away, Tate passing along instructions about reinspecting the entire roof. He never looked her way, increasing the *keep away* vibes, but Mr. Hobbins threw her a perplexed look before walking out the doorway. A whole wealth of confusion and curiosity resided in that glance, but he didn't say anything.

"Yeah, you and me both, buddy," she murmured, conscious of her own confusion and uncertainty. Which seemed to grow with every encounter she had with Tate. Close or not.

Tate's refusal to let her help only increased her curiosity about the third floor. Unfortunately, that was the one area where her impulse control had always been weak. She was smart enough to stay in the kitchen until he had finished barking orders and retired to his office. Now the sound of the ocean waves was punctuated by the pounding of hammers and grating of saws. Only when she deemed it clear did she grab the handle of her suitcase and drag it up the back stairs.

Chagrined at how out of breath the task made her, Willow paused just inside the door to her bedroom for a bit of a rest. The bedroom was not so temporary now, thank goodness. Hopefully Mr. Hobbins would at least raise the room's safety standards by that night. Tate would want to avoid a repeat of this morning just as much as she did.

Next time she might not be able to brush it off as well.

The bed frame had been moved and a ladder set up beneath the hole in the ceiling. A stack of tools and stuff lay nearby. She hefted her suitcase to the dresser top so it wouldn't be in the way. She took out the clothes on hangers, which she'd packed on top, and put them in the closet.

On her way back to her suitcase, voices from the

upper floor caught her attention. It was just the workers talking, but it was a reminder of where she wished she was instead of down here unpacking. After a paranoid glance behind her, Willow inched under the damaged ceiling until she could see into the room above.

Her view was limited, but the first thing to catch her eye was an antique rolltop desk. The dull wood left the impression of years' worth of dust coating it and the slatted chair pulled up close. A couple of boxes occupied the space in front of it, blocking access. Slowly Willow rotated to the right, as if moving too fast might give away her intent.

That was when she caught sight of the trunks, which brought a smile to her face. They weren't new plastic and metal pieces. Oh no. These were the real deal, genuine antiques. Leather and handmade nails, if she was seeing correctly from this far away. That was exactly what she had hoped for…exactly where she needed to look.

If she could just find some paperwork proving how the Kingstons had been involved in the tragic historic event that ended with her family being driven from town, her heart would be satisfied. Her discovery wouldn't be for public consumption, but would serve as validation for the Harden sisters, who were all that was left of their family. If what her great-grandmother suspected was true, their mother's insistence that their family was innocent of the crime would be justified… at least to them.

Her frustration at not being able to go right up burned in her, but greed wasn't very ladylike. The trunks looked like they'd been sitting in the same spot for decades. A few more days wouldn't hurt anything. But if she could find what she was looking for, it would clear her family name. Not that anyone would care but her and her sisters.

Still, it was the principle of the thing.

"Ma'am?"

Willow quickly controlled her instinctive need to either yelp or jump or both. After a deep breath, she turned to the workman who had appeared in the doorway. "Yes?"

"We're about to start cutting the ruined parts out of this here ceiling. I need to get this stuff covered."

"Of course. Let me help you."

He protested, but she kept right on working. At least he couldn't order her to stop like Tate. Between the two of them they quickly tarped the remaining furniture and the antique rug. He did insist on moving her open suitcase into the walk-in closet for her, then left her to continue unpacking with a closed door to keep the construction dust out.

She pulled out a couple of changes of clothes. The rest could wait until her bedroom was complete. But the ticking clock in her head told her to hurry. The new mattress should be delivered within an hour, and she needed to be back downstairs to unlock the gates.

Grabbing a couple of T-shirts, she walked to some

empty shelves. She'd gone only a few feet when she heard a light thud on the carpeted floor. Bending over to get a better look in the dim light of the closet, she quickly straightened back up in shock. An unreasonable fear kept her still for long moments. Logically she knew she was being ridiculous. Still her heart thudded hard in her ears.

Finally she forced herself to bend over and pick the object up from the floor. A ring, to be exact. One she recognized all too well. It had been in her family for generations. Blessed, her auntie called it. Given by a pirate who'd turned respectable to the most desirable woman in all of Savannah. The founding couple of their familial line.

A ring said to bring the woman who wore it true abiding love. So why the heck would anyone think Willow would need it at Sabatini House and pack it in her suitcase when she wasn't looking?

Five

"So…" Willow paused for dramatic effect. "Whose brilliant idea was this?"

She slid the antique emerald ring onto the dining room table at her family's weekly Sunday dinner. Each person sitting around the table received a moment of intense study, except Rosie, who, at only nine months old, couldn't have been involved.

When her older sister, Jasmine, pressed her lips together as if suppressing a smile, Willow had her culprit. "This isn't funny," she complained, wincing at the slight whine in her protest.

Jasmine's fiancé, Royce, had to add his two cents' worth. "We just want to see you as happy as we are," he teased.

"Since when are you buying into this pirate legend business?"

He hugged Jasmine to him. "Why not? I've got the proof right here. After all, your sister wore that ring almost the entire time she worked on planning the masquerade event for me."

"Well, the last thing I need to do is romance my boss," Willow said. Their youngest sister, Ivy, scoffed before pushing back from the table and crossing to the stove. Her back was stiff, giving her a closed-off look.

"You okay, Ivy?" Willow asked.

Her sister didn't respond, which worried Willow. She had always been close with Ivy, even more so since Jasmine had adopted Rosie. Their oldest sister had taken on a huge responsibility and gone through a lot of changes in the last year. Willow and Ivy had turned to each other as confidantes rather than add to their sister's stress.

As she watched Ivy, it occurred to Willow that it had been a couple of weeks since she'd had a good talk with her younger sister. First she'd been preparing for her new job, and then living at Sabatini House had cut back on the time they spent together. She should see if she could have her sister out there. Maybe seeing the awesome house would distract her from whatever was bothering her or give her a chance to open up about it.

Of course, it might take a miracle to talk Tate into letting her have a stranger in the house. She'd better hold off on that conversation for a while.

She turned back to Jasmine and Royce. "He definitely has his own ideas about how things should be done," Willow said. "Where I can go and what I can do. I mean, I realize this is his home, but I'm beginning to think Tate is überparanoid."

Except he didn't give off a paranoid vibe. So she couldn't quite grasp what the issue is. "And being in control is the be-all, end-all for him."

Jasmine cast an arch glance at her fiancé. "Well, men tend to be that way."

"That doesn't mean we're wrong," Royce said, "for all the good it does us." His smile was amused instead of defensive, though.

Jasmine and Royce had clashed about how things should be done from the moment he'd hired her to co-ordinate a charity event for him. As Willow watched them now, she was amazed. For two people who had often butted heads, their love for each other and Jasmine's adopted daughter, Rosie, was palpable.

Of course, they'd overcome a lot to get that way.

"It's just..." Willow struggled to put her feelings about her new job, and her new boss, into words. Though not all her feelings—the last thing she wanted to discuss with Royce was the disturbing amount of lust that colored her every interaction with Tate. "I don't understand. Why is he so defensive? What's he hiding in all those rooms? And what does he do with himself all day? I mean, I know he's a writer. Is he writing all day? About what?" The frustrating lack of answers left her antsy.

Ivy turned away from the stove, where she was putting the finishing touches on the marinara sauce, to ask, "What do you mean?" Her earlier stiffness seemed to be gone.

"Well, after we did the house tour, he went upstairs and I didn't see him again. He just silently appeared almost the minute dinner was on the table."

Ivy snickered. "I can see that driving you crazy."

Meanie. "I just want to know!"

He had to have been locked up in his office all afternoon. She'd never heard him moving around and hadn't seen him the few times she'd gone up to check on the workman in her bedroom. He'd never been in the workout room when she'd gone into the basement to wash the dirty bedclothes. "What was he doing with himself for so many hours on end?"

"Why do you care?" Royce asked. Then he glanced around as the other women laughed. "What?"

"Willow is notoriously curious," Jasmine explained. "So the more Tate Kingston tries to hide things from her, the more she's gonna want to dig."

"I can't help it," Willow protested. "He's just so secretive and closemouthed and..."

"Sexy?" Ivy teased.

"Yes." Willow sighed, lured into the answer by her sister's lighter expression. Then Willow shook her head. "No, no, he's not."

Auntie threw in her two cents' worth while she supervised Rosie in her high chair. "Methinks she protests too much…"

"Auntie!" Willow's cursed pale complexion flushed hotly. "He's frustrating, that's what he is."

"Because he wants to keep his privacy?" Royce asked.

Willow could tell this whole conversation had him confused. Trying to explain it to him when she felt she couldn't be completely open was confusing for Willow, too. The sisters and Auntie had long been on their own and weren't used to male input yet.

Auntie wasn't really their aunt at all. She'd been their mother's nanny when she was little and their grandmother's best friend. Auntie and the Harden sisters had all lived together in this house since their parents had died in a car accident. Until Jasmine had fallen in love with Royce. Then she and Rosie had moved out.

Since the sisters had come to live with Auntie, they'd never had a man in the house. Not a boyfriend or lover or spouse had lived there. It had just been the girls.

Royce's presence changed things. Though Jasmine and Rosie had moved into his penthouse in historic Savannah, they were here as often as not.

Ivy grinned at Willow as she carried the pot of sauce to the table and set it on a trivet. "You know that secrecy means he has some kind of tragic past," she said.

"You are so melodramatic," Willow scoffed, but deep down…

Ivy took her chair with a knowing look. "But I'm right."

Jasmine gasped, theatrically laying her hands over her heart. "I bet if you wore *the ring* you could get him to fall in love with you," she teased. "Then you would know *all* his secrets."

Ivy groaned. The out-of-character response caused Willow to cast her a worried glance. "What's the matter, Ivy? I thought you were a believer in the family ring?"

Jasmine piped up. "I definitely am."

"Oh, hush," Ivy said, and left the room.

"What's the matter with her?" Royce asked, though her disappearance didn't stop him from digging into dinner.

Jasmine smiled, but her expression was a little sad around the edges. "She's a little testy at the moment. The legend of the ring starts with a pirate who found it and used it to win over his true love. She was an upper-class woman who never would have been within his reach before that. But he married her and started our family line."

Royce nodded. "What does that have to do with Ivy? You wore the ring the whole time we were working together, right?"

"Yes, sir." The furrow between Jasmine's brows deepened. "But Ivy wore it the night of the masquerade."

They all fell quiet for a moment. Something had happened between Ivy and her boss on the night of the masquerade ball that Jasmine had planned as a charity fund-raiser for Royce and his company. Only Jasmine and Willow knew that her boss had taken Ivy to his bed. The next morning, he had left to deal with a problem at one of his manufacturing plants. That was three weeks ago. *Bless her heart.*

"I think I'll hold off on wearing the ring," Willow said, turning it over and over in her hand. The lighting caused the teardrop-shaped emerald-and-gold filigree to glitter and spark. Almost to herself she mused, "I've gotten myself in enough trouble already."

"How so?" Jasmine asked.

The last thing Willow wanted to talk about was ending up in Tate's bed or waking up to him wrapped around her body like a real lover. Or what a hard time she was having forgetting those heated moments before he'd woken.

So she chose a safer topic. "My whole purpose in going to Sabatini House didn't have anything to do with Tate. If he keeps everything locked down, I'll have wasted my whole summer on a wild-goose chase."

Not that the memory of Tate's body against hers could ever be considered a waste.

"What are you talking about?" Jasmine asked.

Willow caught Auntie's gaze. "I read the journal."

Out of the corner of her eye, she saw Jasmine and Royce exchange a glance. She figured she better explain before the questions started.

"Auntie gave me our great-grandmother's journal."

"I found it in the attic, in the same trunk as the ring," Auntie interjected.

Willow had spent many a rainy afternoon prowling through the old trunks in their attic with Auntie. It was how she'd come by her love of antiques and mysteries.

"While I was reading the journal, I came across some speculation from great-grandmother about who was really responsible for the tragedy that eventually drove them out of town."

Royce jumped in. "This is about the sabotage of the rival company's ship, right?"

Willow nodded. "The accusation was that our great-grandfather, a direct descendent of a pirate, sunk the biggest ship of a rival by setting it on fire to give his own shipping company an advantage. That family's eldest son and heir was on the ship the night it caught fire and died."

"Great-Grandfather vehemently denied any involvement," Jasmine added, "but no one believed him. The rival family threatened first his business, then his wife and child. He felt he had no choice but to skip town."

Willow drew in a deep breath before saying, "But Great-Grandmother knew there were other shipping companies that would have been happy to get a lead over that same rival. Possibly even the Kingstons."

The others stared at her with wide eyes. Even Rosie seemed to focus in on her, as if sensing something wasn't right in her world.

"Oh, Willow," Jasmine finally breathed. "Please be careful."

Willow shrugged off her concern. "It's just a piece of history now. At least, to most people. But it's our history. I, for one, would like to know the truth."

"I don't know about this," Royce said.

"I do," Willow said. "Our family history means a lot to me. And that truth just might be hiding in a trunk on Sabatini House's third floor. I want to find it."

The question remained, was she willing to defy Tate Kingston to find her answers?

Willow set his plate in front of him on the table in silence. She didn't offer any pleasantries with the food. Of course, he didn't, either.

Tate had gone out of his way to get this situation back to strictly business. It didn't help him forget the feel of Willow's body against his, but at least a professional attitude kept him from reaching for her whenever she walked by him.

He kept all answers precise and as short as possible. Small talk wasn't an issue…he wasn't good at that anyway. And he certainly never addressed anything personal. She probably thought he hated her—and that was best for everyone.

So why did the thought unsettle him?

There were other things that also left him off-kilter. For instance, he'd started to notice little touches around the house—homey touches. A pillow here. A new picture there. Yesterday he'd come across a little clock that had been his mother's, fully restored, on the mantel in the living room. Whether Willow believed it or not, he did actually prowl the house. Usually in the dark hours of the night.

There it had sat, pretty as you please, right below his eye level. He'd wanted to curse Willow for the memories she'd evoked, but he couldn't stop himself from walking over to it. Touching the little clock that had been his mother's had been beyond him, but he had to check for dents, chips in the delicate paint. Any signs of the years of neglect he'd allowed to occur.

All had been well…but not with his soul.

He'd wanted to fire her, but by morning the feeling had passed. She'd be gone at the end of the summer… and he'd be free of the temptation to kiss those freckles on her face. Or spark that redheaded temper so he could see the tension enter her body until it radiated from her.

Until then, he'd stay far, far away.

So why, when he saw her pass by the doorway with a covered plate and a book, did he ask, "Where are you going?"

Her glance his way was too brief for him to get a good look into those glassy green eyes.

"To eat lunch. Don't worry. I'll be back."

He wasn't worried—exactly. And her cautious tone would have been funny if he hadn't been the one to put it there. The word *cautious* just didn't seem to describe Willow. Tate saw her as more of a free spirit—a fiery, determined sprite who knew exactly what she wanted and would plow right over anyone in the way...or when the situation warranted, sneak around the boundaries anyone set up for her.

But he had a good view of the rest of her...and the book under her elbow. His heart started pounding out of his control.

"You don't seem like the horror story type," he said. The words slipped out before the "business only" side of him could kick in.

She paused, then turned back to him as if she wasn't quite sure he was speaking to her. She offered a half grin that looked sad on her full lips. "I get that a lot." She mimicked a high-pitched tone. "What would an innocent-looking thing like you want to read that scary stuff for?" She shrugged her delicate shoulders. "I love it, though."

"Me, too." More than she would ever know. Yep, this could end up very bad.

"Really?" she asked, her eyes going wide and finally meeting his. "I love it. Horror, mystery, suspense. Anything that keeps me guessing."

His smile was genuine for once. "You aren't one of those obnoxious people who guess the ending all the time, are you? And ruin it for everybody else?"

"Of course not. And if I can guess the ending, then the author isn't trying hard enough."

He shouldn't ask. He knew he shouldn't. "What about him?" he asked, nudging his chin toward the book. As he waited for her answer, his stomach did a slow roll that brought on a surge of nausea.

Maybe it was a sign of weakness, but it wasn't every day that he got to meet one of his fans. Okay, he'd never done it on *any* day. Except for his agent, and then his editor, Tate had never spoken face-to-face with someone who enjoyed his writing. They were professionals. True fans were a little different.

Willow was his first.

Luckily she didn't notice anything unusual. "Oh, Adam Tate is one of my favorite authors. He combines historical facts with suspense and supernatural horror elements. All of the books are set in famous places where major events have happened, with all these fascinating details. And he's pretty accurate, I might add."

"Oh?"

"Yep…" The smirk on her lips drew his gaze. "I'm a history teacher. Remember?"

"Right!" But Tate was having trouble concentrating. The excitement on her face was utterly fascinating. Why was he doing this to himself? "And the stories keep you guessing?"

"Definitely." She frowned, wrinkling her normally smooth forehead. "Tate, are you okay?"

He swallowed against the nausea. "Of course. Why?"

"You look funny."

Uh-oh. "No. I'm fine."

He turned back to the table. Reclaiming his seat, he forced himself to keep his gaze trained on his plate.

Luckily, Willow didn't say anything else. A minute later he heard the door open, then close. He'd probably offended her by abruptly cutting off their conversation. It was the best thing, though—keeping her at arm's length.

Now he knew he had even more he needed to keep from her. He'd never shared his pen name with anyone except his publisher. Even his parents hadn't known. Tate hadn't sought publication until after they had both passed away. Writing was Tate's one pleasure left in this world—the only indulgence he allowed himself.

Besides, if Willow ever knew the real him, the real secrets he hid, she would hate him. Just like his parents had. And it had been every bit deserved.

He glanced out at the sea crashing on the beach within sight of the house. It was his anchor, his reminder. Not in a good way. Oh no. The sight of it, the sound of it beneath the house's foundation, was an eternal reminder that pleasure was something he didn't deserve. Neither was friendship, love or fulfillment. His brother would never have any of those things…so neither would Tate.

He'd been fine with that until Willow came. His parents had never forced him outside of his self-imposed prison—probably because they agreed with him. Oh, they'd never come out and said it. But he knew.

After all, they'd lost two sons that day, all because of his selfish pride. Adam. Then Tate. After that, they'd stayed away more than they were home, though, so Tate hadn't had to come face-to-face with their accusations often. Murdoch had simply followed in his mother's footsteps, never questioning Tate's decision or boundaries.

But Willow did.

Tate turned back to his plate, trying to concentrate on the food. Normally it wasn't a problem. Willow was a great cook. Most of the food was simple and hearty, but delicious. Today, though, too many thoughts distracted him.

Out of the corner of his eye, he saw a movement out the window. A movement that didn't belong to the normal sway of the sea grass and barren tree limbs. Turning his head, he caught sight of a slim figure crossing the sand toward the water.

No!

Willow carried her plate and book, along with what looked like a small blanket. So benign. So innocent. Walking right into dangerous territory.

Tate stood, his heart pumping as fear tried to take hold. *Don't go near the water. Don't get any closer.*

To his relief, she spread the small blanket well away from the water line. But his heart didn't stop racing, even though she picked up her paperback and started to read. Every so often she'd put some food in her mouth. Tate's lunch sat forgotten and cold on the table. He couldn't take his eyes from her, afraid of what might happen if he moved away.

Twenty minutes later, just as he'd come to accept that

she was okay, she set the book on top of the already-finished plate.

She'll pack up and come inside. She has to.

Only she didn't. Leaving her stuff there, she dug her bare feet into the sand as she stood. Stretched. Tate's hands curled into fists.

Don't. Don't do it.

Defying his mental commands with just as much attitude as she showed when defying his verbal ones, she took step after step toward the water's edge. Tate pressed his palms tight against the glass, not sure whether he was actually yelling or if the sound was simply reverberating in his head.

Completely oblivious to his shouts and banging on the window, Willow paused to inspect something in the sand before continuing forward. His voice went hoarse with the strain. He was caught in a slow-motion night-mare despite the daylight.

As her delicate toes met the edge of the rushing water, images flashed through Tate's mind of a young man built strong and utterly familiar with that beach. A young man who rushed the waves as Tate watched from this very window twenty years ago. He had run against the tide until knee-deep, then dived under the incoming waves, seeking the exercise that would cool his anger.

His strong-armed stroke through the choppy sea had been Tate's last glimpse of his brother.

As Tate stood at that same window, his body re-played the terror and fear that had filled him in those last moments of his brother's life. He couldn't block it out, couldn't ignore it. He simply pressed the heels of his hands hard against the glass as he endured. Sweat broke out on his brow. His stomach churned. Desperately his mind sought a way out of the maelstrom. And then it came to him. A whisper at first. A tendril of peace that grew until it formed a hazy wall between him and the tragedy in his mind.

The feel of a woman. A body close against his, the contradiction of contentment and excitement when waking wrapped around Willow. In this memory there was no dread, there was no pain. Nothing had ever done that for him before. *No one* had ever done that.

A different kind of adrenaline rushed against the current inside him, redirecting the river of pain in his memories. Building, turning the tide to an energy Tate didn't want to acknowledge, but truly couldn't resist.

Suddenly he was running out of the house and through the rough sand to Willow. The feel of the grains against the soles of his feet brought back thoughts of another panicked run to the water's edge. Forcefully he blanked his mind and focused on the woman knee-deep in the water ahead of him.

He had to reach her. He would reach her. He would save her.

His low growl carried to her on the wind. Just as he reached the water's edge, she glanced over her shoulder. Surprise opened her features but couldn't save her.

Her sudden surge deeper into the water was no match for his long stride.

Somehow he found his arms around her waist. Without further thought he lifted her, draping her waist across his shoulder. His instincts brought his arms across her thighs, pinning her to him. On the outer edge of his consciousness he could hear her protests, but they didn't register. All he knew was that he had to get her away from the water.

And he had to be close to her.

He slashed back out of the surf. He stomped back across the sand. Now the memories couldn't reach him. His emotions were too strong. He embraced the surge of adrenaline and desire, letting it overtake his primal mind and crowd out the painful images that lurked in the shadows.

He followed a different wave this time, the wave of instinct that drove him to her. He carried her through the door and into the kitchen. Deft movements pulled her back upright and plopped her bottom onto the marble top of the kitchen island.

He recognized the look on her face as one that many a professor over the years had adopted. A *what the hell do you think you're doing?* expression that many people get when working with freshmen at college. Only this time Tate was the one in for the reprimand.

"What the heck was that?" Willow demanded.

Honestly he thought she showed remarkable restraint, but language wasn't a working function of his brain at the moment. He couldn't talk about this right now. Instead he acted.

He buried his hands in that thick auburn hair and pulled her forward until their mouths met. Her body went still against his. Not stiff, but still, expectant, waiting for what was to come. As if she had been waiting for this moment just as much as he had.

Deep inside Tate searched for a thread of restraint, but it was now out of his reach. His mouth opened over hers, his tongue plunging deep. Taking what he wanted, taking what he needed. No more words. Only every ounce of what she could make him feel.

Six

Willow's rational brain demanded an explanation. After all, this was the least professional behavior that she could imagine. Being slung over her boss's shoulder like he was a caveman carrying her back to his cave was completely inappropriate.

If utterly thrilling.

But the anger and determination on his face when he reached her in the water had nothing to do with his being her employer. Frankly, the emotions on his face had been so intense as to scare her.

Then he carried her back here and kissed her more thoroughly than she'd ever been kissed before. She should have resisted. But all too quickly the feel of his mouth against hers drowned out all logical thought.

Until the only thing left was her body's desire to pull him closer. Her mouth's desire to take all that he was willing to give.

Suddenly she felt the light scrape of his nails down her back through her thin shirt. Shivers radiated out from the contact. Without permission, she began to squirm on the marble countertop. Tentatively she stroked her tongue over his.

With a low growly noise, Tate clutched her closer. Her breasts crushed against his chest. His firm hold allowed him to rub against the front of her body. Somehow her knees had parted and Tate now stood between them. The ache at the apex of her thighs told Willow she wanted him closer, then closer still.

No thoughts intruded on the fiery lick of passion. No recriminations nor regrets. Only the driving need for this man, unlike anything she'd ever felt before. Willow wasn't led by her passions. Instead her brain normally ruled the roost, yet somehow in this moment it had taken a permanent vacation.

The whole lower half of her body throbbed. No matter what was going on here, she only wanted to experience the feel of Tate against her once more. And the feel of him inside her for the first time.

He must have wanted the same, because suddenly there was a whoosh of fabric and her thin cotton top was cast aside. Clad in only her underclothes and a light skirt, Willow should have felt self-conscious. Instead she was all too glad when Tate's strong hands explored her heated skin. She clutched him closer as his fingers roughly explored the muscles in her back before making deft work of her bra clasp.

Only then did he allow even a hint of space between them. Their moans filled the kitchen as Tate slid her bra up so he could massage the firm mounds of her breasts. The feel was exquisite, causing her nipples to tighten. Greedy, she wanted more, but couldn't find the words to ask.

Tate seemed to be in too much of a hurry to ask, too. Just as he had with her shirt, he burrowed his hand beneath her skirt. The rough glide of his calloused fingertips against her thighs made her gasp. Sparks radiated from the point of touch to sensitize the skin all over her body. He didn't slow down until he found his way blocked by the elastic edge of her panties.

Then he stilled. The only sound in the room was the mingling of their harsh gasps for air. Though how Willow could hear even that over the pounding of her blood in her ears was a miracle. The last thing she wanted was to face reality, but the longer Tate refused to move, the more self-consciousness crept in. The more Willow became aware what she was doing was a big mistake.

Tilting her head back, she forced her eyelids to open. The face before hers was a frozen picture of anguish and need. Tate's classic dark features were a study in the struggle he obviously felt. Suddenly his jaw clenched hard. Down below, his fingers dug into the sensitive juncture between her thighs.

After long moments, he finally tilted his head down. When his eyes opened, she gasped at the intensity of the passion within their dark depths. Even as his mouth returned to hers, blotting out reality, his fingers grasped her panties and tore them with a harsh tug.

Her core melted as he jerked her forward to the edge. The V of her legs left her exposed and vulnerable. Not for long. She felt a vague fumbling between them, then Tate stepped forward those last few inches. His big body forced her legs even farther apart, but there was no time to feel vulnerable. Instead a determined exploration of his fingers gave way to blunt pressure at her core. Her body resisted for long moments, moments that reminded her just how long it had been since she'd accepted anyone into her body this way. A slight pumping motion helped him gain headway, spreading her juices over the smooth head of him.

One hand snaked behind her, pulling her closer, gaining him access. He buried the other in her hair. His mouth covered hers, his thrusting tongue mimicking the movements of his lower body. Willow's mind overloaded on bliss. The repeated thrusts conquered every inch of her passage, stretching her tight. Friction sparked electricity that tingled in her nipples and tight nub. She cried out with every stroke, her hands clutching his biceps. Urging him closer, faster, harder.

His entire body pressed up and then back. The feel of him saturated her consciousness from her thighs to her palms to her breasts. She sucked his hot, masculine scent deep into her lungs. Each thrust brought him close enough for her to press her lips against his neck and taste the steamy essence of the Tate he'd hidden from her all this time.

With a roar, he ground against her. The hard pulse of him inside her caused her own ecstasy to explode. They strained against each other, draining every last ounce of pleasure they could draw from the connection.

Until neither of them could do anything but gasp and groan.

Only long moments later did Willow become aware of the change in Tate's body. He stiffened, and a half groan, half self-deprecating choke came from his throat.

Reality had returned in an instant.

Unfortunately it found Willow with her naked bottom on her employer's kitchen island and no dignified way to extract herself from this situation. Because that wasn't a sound someone made when they were happy and satisfied. Oh no. At least he hadn't removed all of her clothes, so she had that small dignity.

"That was incredible..." Tate groaned.

What? Just as Willow relaxed, he went on. "Incredibly stupid."

All the tension of the last few minutes coalesced into a ball of nerves setting up a protest inside her stomach. Without thought, Willow pushed hard at his arms. Tate released her immediately, not trying to contain her. He backed up willingly, with no protest.

Willow slid from the high counter with difficulty,

struggling to keep her skirt down out of a belated sense of modesty. Then she backed slowly away, step by step. She fumbled with her bra, struggling to get it back down over her breasts. Her mind, heart and body were too caught up in turmoil to even form coherent thoughts.

She couldn't look up at him, not even when he whispered her name. Her back bumped against the door frame, and she fumbled behind her for empty space. A quick glance at his face revealed the same wide-eyed surprise mixed with chaos that she felt inside. But she didn't stick around to share.

Acting completely on instinct she threw herself out the door, racing for the staircase.

Well, that hadn't gone according to plan.

Tate's goal had been strictly professional behavior. He'd been aiming for almost cold, almost impersonal. How he'd gotten from that to his current conundrum was a complete mystery to him.

A combination of dismay and satisfaction swept through him as he glanced down to see the ruined remains of Willow's panties on the floor. Chauvinistic though it may be… Hypocritical though it definitely was… Tate had to acknowledge the heat that rekindled inside of him with the knowledge that he would keep that small reminder.

He picked up the scrap and slid it quickly into his pocket, as if it didn't really happen if no one saw him. Then he circled the island to clean up at the sink. He didn't want to think about what had occurred. And he didn't want to think about how much he wanted the proof that it had.

It wasn't until he held the towel in his hand with his unbuttoned pants still around his hips that he realized something was very wrong.

The adrenaline that coursed through him now was true panic—pure and simple. As he turned and raced down the hall and up the stairs, he clenched his hands against the unwanted emotions.

I can fix this. I can fix this.

He stormed through the door into Willow's bedroom, only to find it empty. So much chaos churned inside him that for a moment he couldn't grasp the fact she wasn't there. He crossed to the bathroom door, only to find just enough self-control not to blow it off its hinges. Pressure built inside as he pounded on the wood separating him from Willow. The bitter taste of regret flooded his mouth.

"Willow!"

Just when he thought about breaking the door down, he heard the click of the latch. The door swung open on a woman whose auburn hair was in disarray and red-rimmed eyes burned with fire. Tate refused to register with that might mean.

"What the hell—" she started.

"We made a mistake."

Apparently that was the wrong approach.

"We?" One brow arched high as she glanced down at his crotch. Her sharp tone brought him up short.

Old instincts immediately kicked in—a lifetime of protecting himself against the aggression of others. It was the way his family had operated since the beginning, from what he could tell. The turmoil and uneasiness of this unusual situation gave Tate permission to slide right into the comfortable role.

"If you think this is all on me, you're mistaken," he asserted. "I didn't hear any protest from your direction when I had you on the kitchen counter."

A bright pink flush started at her neck and quickly spread up and over her cheeks. Tate actually felt the urge to step back. He didn't know Willow as well as he should, but he had a feeling that was a very bad sign.

But she didn't yell as he expected. Instead she set him straight through teeth clenched so tight she'd have a headache later, he was sure.

"Are you seriously banging on my door so you can make sure I know this was my fault?"

Her escalating volume urged him to move, to speak, do something. He opened his mouth, but she didn't give him a chance to defend his stupidity.

"I *did* protest," she insisted. Striding forward, she actually crowded him back across the room. And he was gentleman enough to let her…this time. "Long before we ever got to the kitchen. All the way back to the house. *You* are the one who wouldn't listen. *You* are the one who pulled the caveman act."

"*You* shouldn't have gone in the water. It's off-limits for a reason. You should have known that."

Willow cocked her head to the side. "Let me get this straight…all of this happened because the ocean, the very body of water that surrounds this island, that this house is actually built on, is *off-limits*?"

The rising anger in her voice and the use of air quotes edged her into dangerous territory. The redheaded temper was a real thing. A lifetime of fighting back urged Tate to retaliate, but he had just enough intelligence left to realize he'd get nowhere. He had to calm her down before she'd listen.

Unsure of his next move, he simply let her blow off steam.

"I protested plenty while slung over your shoulder, he-man." She poked his chest with a short finger. He let her because he was not proud of that behavior now, outside of the haze of desire. "You are the one who kissed me, remember?"

Finally Tate grasped her hand. Without intending to, he curled his fingers around hers until some of her stiffness melted. Quietly he admitted, "I remember."

How could he forget? The taste of her, the smell of her. He would swear everything about Willow was designed to be his own personal kryptonite. He didn't want to notice how her breasts moved with each breath, or how full her lips were after she'd kissed him. So why did he?

And the situation they were in now was the very

reason he needed to stay far, far away. He released her and deliberately moved closer to the door, to freedom.

"Look, I didn't come here to make accusations or blame you for what happened."

"Could have fooled me."

Tate tamped down his instinct to tear into her. She didn't deserve that. And he was better than that, better than his ingrained family traits. "We have a problem, Willow."

"I'm sure you do."

Tate was done with the hysterics. It was time to figure this out, to find a solution. He looked her straight in the eye with a stern expression.

"Willow, I didn't use a condom."

Seven

Tate would hate for her to lock herself in the bathroom again. But Willow couldn't find it in herself to care. She needed time to process how to fix the mess they'd landed themselves in. As far as she was concerned, the conversation was over when he harshly insisted on knowing if she was on birth control.

As if that demand was the response she'd been expecting after the most incredible sexual experience of her life.

She also didn't expect him to go away and leave her alone, but that's exactly what he did. After half an hour of silence, she poked her head out of the bathroom to find her bedroom empty, the door closed.

Miracle of miracles, as Auntie would say.

Willow flopped down on her bed, but her body remained tense. She was waiting for Tate to come barging
in again. She couldn't think about the lack of a condom,
or the possible consequences.

Instead she focused on the practical. What should
she do now? Leave? Stay?

Facing Tate every day after making love to him and
pretending it never happened wasn't something she
could handle. Knowing he saw it as a mistake, a com-
plication, when she'd experienced something far different would be unbearable...

No, she couldn't stay.

She allowed herself the luxury of a few tears before
dragging herself from the bed. The pounding headache
brought on by the rapid flux of emotions only added
to her misery. But she forced herself to start opening
drawers and emptying them onto the bed in neat little
piles. She'd go home...even if that was the immature
thing to do.

After about an hour, she heard steps approaching
from Tate's wing. He paused outside her door.

She stared at the handle, anticipating the turn. The
nerves tightening her stomach only made her headache
worse. There was almost a feeling like any noise from
her would cause him to barge through that door. She
didn't dare move. But long minutes later he continued
on, leaving her to collapse on the last available space
on her bed in relief.

She'd just started to drift off when the sound of a

motor disturbed her. It was so unusual on the island that her foggy mind struggled for a moment to identify it. Dragging her weary body to the window, she saw Tate drive the house's Jeep out across an unknown path instead of down the drive. From Murdoch's notes, she knew the unfamiliar road led to the airplane hangar on the other side of the island. For some reason Murdoch hadn't explained, Tate didn't take the car on the rare occasions he left the island. His only method of transport away from Sabatini House was his plane. Murdoch had used the Jeep to handle all of the travel to Savannah for household necessities.

Was Tate going to blow off steam by working on his plane? Or fly for a while, the way some people would go for a drive? Her answer came about thirty minutes later when she heard his four-seater plane take off. She reached the window in just enough time to see it lift over the trees, curve in a graceful arc, then disappear out of her line of sight.

Where was he going? Especially this late in the evening. But Willow was too tired to figure it out. Instead she sprawled on her bed next to her packed suitcase and let sleep obliterate all the questions and her headache.

When she woke, darkness had fully arrived and the clock said it was just after eight at night. Somehow she knew Tate wasn't back, but she padded out to the garage and confirmed the Jeep wasn't there.

As she walked back to the house and glanced up at its grandeur, even in the darkness of the summer night, her heart spasmed. In all the drama, she'd forgotten one of her main reasons for coming to Sabatini House.

The third floor.

She rushed back inside. Why, oh why, had she fallen asleep? She needed to find the keys.

Where had Tate gotten them from the other day to let the workmen up to the third floor? The utility room off the kitchen. She remembered seeing him come out of there. She only hoped he'd put them back where he got them from and not dropped them in his office or something.

After fifteen minutes of searching the drawers, she opened the cabinet and found a pegboard with several sets of keys. She quickly grabbed the one marked Third Floor, then rushed for the stairs.

As she worked the key into the lock, she glanced to the side to see an open door. Light from the hall showed letters stenciled onto the wall. Not a poem or a quote, but the ABCs.

Like for a nursery.

She shouldn't open the door. She really shouldn't. But still she reached out to push it back, letting the hall light spill into the darkened room.

She flipped the light switch, but only a single bulb in the huge room lit up, leaving lots of gray shadows clouding the space. Gorgeous built-in bookcases with filigreed edges lined one wall. The shelves were filled to the brim with hardback books, but no pictures or personal memorabilia. Large toys that would now be considered antiques were scattered throughout the open space. Some of it was covered like the furniture downstairs, but she could make out a couple of handmade rocking horses, a large wooden playhouse shaped like a pirate ship and two tricycles. An open chest under one window overflowed with painted building blocks. Bins marked Toys or Clothes were stacked in one corner, partially concealed by a tarp.

Willow wandered farther in, fascinated by the abandoned nature of the space. Even though it was filled with stuff, there was no sense of any of the occupants who had previously lived and played here. Even though the items were personal in nature, the arrangement was more of a storage area. Yet some things looked as if the owner had simply walked away from them one day. Weird.

She passed a large oversize bassinet filled with neglected stuffed toys. Involuntarily, she rubbed her hand over a fluffy elephant dressed in a sailor suit.

The sight that stopped her short was a crib. No, not one crib. Two cribs, pushed together so their sturdy hand-carved railings almost touched. She stared for a moment, trying to figure out the puzzle. A quick glance into a second open area of the room revealed two twin beds and dressers on opposite walls. The beds were neatly covered with navy comforters decorated with sailboats. As if someone had simply gotten the children up, made their beds and walked out yesterday, except for the layer of dust covering them and more boxes lining the wall.

From what she could tell, Sabatini House hadn't had children in it since, well, Tate. Had it? Crossing to one of the dressers, she picked up a simple photograph, the only one she could see in the entire space. For having so much stuff, the room was oddly stark. No family photographs lining the mantel: no baby pictures, no cute little bathtub photo ops. Were the mementos all packed away?

Only this single framed photograph still remained. She rubbed the dusty glass to get a better look. It had been taken in a photography studio and showed two little boys in smart white sailor suits with navy decorations. Two dark-haired, dark-eyed boys with the same full, definitively shaped lips as Tate's.

"What are you doing in here?"

Willow twisted around to find Tate behind her, his face tight and menacing.

"Tate! You scared me."

Something about being in this room, seeing everything that had meant so much to him and his brother, and knowing the eventual outcome, deepened the darkness of his mood.

"I told you to stay out of the rooms." He almost said she knew the rooms were off-limits, but the last thing he wanted was to bring back the memory of her teasing him about the use of that phrase.

Thoughts of their lighter moments, thoughts of the easily lit attraction she held for him, made him want to rage at the universe. As if he hadn't martyred himself enough, the world saw fit to bring him this incredible temptation. He knew good and well he was supposed to look and not touch. As usual, touching hadn't turned out so well, had it?

Not realizing just how dangerous he was, she quickly fired back.

"Actually," she said, adopting the stubborn look that made her sparse spattering of freckles stand out. "You told me to stay out of the third floor. I'm not on the third floor."

"Touché."

He stared directly at her, almost afraid of what he'd find in this room. He probably hadn't been in here in a good five years if not more. Though it was easier than going into his brother's last bedroom.

But that door was currently locked, unlike this one.

When she raised her brow, Tate knew he'd stretched the moment too long. Forcing himself to glance around, he noted as if for the first time that everything had been stored in sets of two. A dead giveaway. Had she divined his secret already?

"And what did you find so interesting in here?"

She hesitated only a moment before answering. "Honestly, it's hard to imagine Sabatini House with a nursery." Her voice softened as she, too, looked around, the framed photograph in her hand forgotten for the moment. That was one thing Tate refused to acknowledge.

"It should be. The Kingstons have never been well-known for their softer side."

"What do you mean?"

Her voice seemed to come from the very shadows of the room. Under normal circumstances, the last thing Tate would do was indulge her curiosity. But maybe letting her in on some of Sabatini House's secrets would be for the best. She should know exactly what this family was like—it would help win her over to his way of thinking regarding the encounter they'd had in the kitchen.

"Every last one of us was born from the loins of a pirate. Not the well-known kind here in Savannah. Not the watered-down version who loved to drink, enjoyed women, and roamed the seas far and wide. Oh no."

Tate swallowed hard, stomach churning as he contemplated his heritage. "We come from the bloodthirsty, ice-cold kind. The kind that roamed the seas to kill for sport, to take what didn't belong to him. For my ancestor, that included his wife, who belonged to someone else."

He wasn't sure why he smiled. Surely the expression looked as grim as he felt. "He brought her here to this island and started his dynasty, determined to be the best in the shipping industry that was rapidly growing. He wanted to be a respectable man—but had not-so-respectable practices. He was ruthless and went after anything he wanted, staying just on the right side of the law. He was exceptional at not getting caught.

"His wife gave him three sons, a single and a set of twins. Each generation since has had another set of twins. My brother and I were identical."

"Where is he?" she asked, her voice barely more than a whisper.

"Adam is dead," Tate said starkly, "and it's all my fault."

"Why?"

He liked that she didn't protest…didn't throw out platitudes to try to make him feel better.

"Because I did what we always do. I took what I wanted without caring how he felt about it. And he died. I lived."

His father and grandfather would have called that survival of the fittest. Tate saw it as perpetuating the bad things in the world…drowning out the good.

The atmosphere in the abandoned room drew out his next words. "Some days I wonder if the universe took him on purpose. Regardless, his death taught me something. There will be no marriage, no children, no future for me. When I die, this family is done."

He stubbornly shook off whatever hold the memories had over him and focused hard on the woman in front of him. "That's why I want you to take this." He pulled a flat packet from the back pocket of his jeans.

Willow squinted in the dim light. "What is it?"

"A morning-after pill."

Even in the shadows he could see her eyes go wide, exposing the whites. "Are you serious?"

"As serious as possible." She needed to understand the gravity of the situation.

"I'm sorry, Tate. I can't."

He didn't get mad, didn't rage. But she'd soon learn he could be as stubborn as her.

The emotions inside him urged him forward, deliberate steps that carried him closer until he loomed over her. "Then you will stay here until you see why this is necessary. Because the Kingston family ends with me."

Eight

Unease over the whole situation stalked Willow, leaving her to toss and turn in her bed the entire night while she tried to think through her options. Morning did not find her happy or any closer to a decision. Tate's stoic, almost silent pressure didn't help.

After his declaration, she'd expected him to badger her into doing what he wanted ASAP. Instead he'd rarely said a word to her today. He simply watched her, but that pointed gaze spoke everything he wouldn't say out loud.

If he'd known anything about her—which she was starting to doubt—she was a woman with a need to know. She liked facts, history and knowledge for its own sake. If Tate thought she was swallowing a pill without any other information, he was sadly mistaken.

She simply wasn't sure how to tell him this. The reasons were pretty private. And though she'd shared her body with him, Tate's arm's-length attitude didn't encourage her to share her thoughts.

Dates had been few and far between for Willow. She was a little too bookish for most men, or so she gathered. At least compared with the party-hearty college students she was surrounded by on a daily basis.

Few dates meant even fewer sexual partners, which was why she'd never bothered taking a birth control pill. Why mess with Mother Nature if she wasn't bothering anyone?

Willow had always insisted on a condom before because she was practical, after all. The fact that she'd never even thought about it with Tate left her deeply dismayed. What had happened between them was different, far more explosive than she'd ever experienced with the few other men she'd allowed that close.

Considering their current stalemate, she couldn't believe that part of her wanted to repeat the experience. But the fiercely passionate and possessive Tate had been so much more dynamic than the one staring balefully at her across the kitchen island the next morning. Or should she call it the scene of the crime? She'd never see this kitchen quite the same again.

Not that she would be seeing it again. Not if she had anything to say about it.

"I'm not arguing with you. You're not leaving."

She glanced over at the suitcase she'd brought down

from her room. "Tate, I think it's for the best. This is... uncomfortable."

"It won't be forever."

His brutal disregard made her temper flare and face flush, but she clenched her fist to regain control. "I won't be bullied, Tate."

"Honey, if I was a bully, this conversation wouldn't be nearly this civil. It really wouldn't be a conversation at all. Instead, I'm simply demanding you stay until we've come to a mutually agreed upon conclusion."

Though the words sounded conciliatory, Willow had a feeling he still meant his way or else. Why, oh why, had she let herself be put in this position?

He stepped closer, bracing his hands on the island. She wouldn't think about what had happened on it just yesterday. Or how good it had felt to have him inside her. Since she now had to live with this churning chaos in her gut that wouldn't give her the answer that would fix everything.

"This is not a family you want to bring children into, Willow," he insisted, as if that were the only issue on the table. "My ancestors laughed while they ruined their competitors in business, took women they wanted without thought or permission, cheated their employees out of their wages. Hell—my parents weren't above using those same psycho games with their own children— pitting us against each other until one of us was dead. Not that they noticed he was gone."

Willow watched Tate wide-eyed, her attention

snagged by the return of real emotions to his expression. She almost gasped from the intensity of his words and the anguish on his face. How did he live every day with all of that hidden behind his usual tightly controlled facade?

She was beginning to realize that was exactly what it was—just a facade.

"How did he die?" she whispered. For some reason, it was important for her to know. As if the answer was a key that would unlock the puzzle before her.

Tate's gaze flicked behind her to the window in the breakfast nook. For a moment she thought he would avoid answering her. Then she realized he was giving her a clue as he said, "In the same water you so innocently waded into yesterday."

Willow's chest tightened, cutting off her breath for a moment. She remembered dipping her toes into the cool, lapping waves. Heaven help her.

"We'd had an argument," Tate continued, his voice low and intense. "Adam went swimming—alone—to blow off some steam. He never came back."

His brother. His twin. How awful. She wanted to ask how it felt to lose someone who was literally the other half of you—but she didn't dare. Tate shouldn't have to relive the emotions, the pain. Though his expression told her he relived it more often than necessary.

His pain made her own heart hurt. She couldn't stop herself from reaching over the island to cover his hand with her own. "I'm so sorry, Tate."

His eyes widened for a moment, as if he didn't know what to make of this simple offer of comfort. Or, heaven forbid, he had never been offered comfort before now. What kind of family left a young man to suffer the guilt of his twin's death without trying to reassure him that it wasn't his fault? That he didn't make his twin go into the ocean alone, and certainly didn't cause whatever had led to his drowning, no matter how angry he'd been at the moment.

As a child she'd spent many nights crying over the deaths of her parents, but she'd been surrounded by a family that cared about her, talked through these things with her and helped her process the tragedy. Obviously no one had ever done that with Tate.

Sounded like he knew his family pretty well when he warned her about them.

He'd bared his soul to her...or as close as she'd imagined he could come to it. She at least owed him an explanation. "I don't just want to leave because of—"

She glanced down at the cool marble of the kitchen island. What should she say? *Because we had sex? Because you want to force me to do what? Prevent further consequences?* Her cheeks burned over all of those options, but she ignored her reaction. Maybe he would, too.

She noticed he'd dropped his dark, brooding gaze to the counter and his right index finger tapped heavily against the surface. Was he thinking the same things she was?

He didn't make her wait to find out. "Do you think I can't control myself? Is that why you want to leave? After yesterday's display, that's understandable. But I can keep my hands to myself—I assure you."

Willow didn't want him to, but that was a desire she would keep to herself. Instead, despite her embarrassment, she would suck it up and talk to him about her misgivings. She discussed difficult subjects with her students all the time...it was just easier because it wasn't personal. Still...she could do this.

"Tate, do you realize you are demanding I do something to my body that I have no clue about?"

He cocked his head to the side and frowned. She was fascinated how his entire face was involved when he let down his guard—brows lowering, eyes narrowing, forehead wrinkling. She usually had to search for clues about his emotional state.

"It's perfectly safe," he said.

Willow took a deep breath, choosing her words carefully. "I'm sure it is, but I don't know that—for certain. I've never looked into this—well, I've never needed to know before. But now I do." When he continued to look at her with that confused frown, she shrugged. "How does it work? What are the side effects?"

"Doesn't it come with all of that information?"

Was he really this dense? He looked genuinely perplexed, but she had to wonder. "Have you ever tried to read the inserts that come with medicine?" she challenged.

She could tell he hadn't but wouldn't admit it.

"Most of the words don't make any sense…and I have multiple college degrees."

"So, look it up."

His stubborn nonchalance had her slapping her hands on her hips. "On what, exactly?"

Comprehension finally dawned. She could see it come over his face like a sunrise. Without warning, Tate left the room, leaving her to fume over his lack of realization that she'd been taken back to the 1980s, technology-wise. Yes, they lived in an age where the most common way to find out what she needed was to search the internet. But she hadn't counted on being held captive in a house where the only computer was in his office—and thus, off-limits—and her Wi-Fi wouldn't work.

For an author, he sure hadn't thought this scenario through.

The sound of his footsteps allowed her to track his movements through the house. The tide was out for the day, muting the sound of rushing water that served as the soundtrack for everything here at Sabatini House. She lost track of him on the second floor, but heard the slam of his office door after a few moments.

It wasn't long before he came back to the kitchen with a small stack of papers, which he'd obviously just printed from the computer. He held them out to her. "Here you go."

She glanced down at the top page. The headline was

about the medication followed by several paragraphs of text. Looked like she wasn't the only one overly fond of research.

She stood there, staring down at the papers, and realized how awkward this entire situation was. But now that most everything was out in the open, she felt better. Then she thought about all that he'd told her in the last day. "I'm sorry, Tate," she said, barely able to look up at him. "No one should ever have to grow up like that."

His expression immediately closed down. "If it's in my power, no one else will."

A few days later, Willow very casually picked up her covered plate and book, then headed for the outer door.

"Where are you going?" Tate demanded.

His gruff tone made her want to jump, but she wasn't about to give Tate an edge. She refused to meet his gaze—just shot a smile in his general direction.

"I'm eating my lunch."

Then she confidently strode out the door. For the last several days, she'd silently insisted on returning to the beach to have her lunch every day. Tate never tried to stop her, but she could feel his gaze on her most of the time.

Some people would think she was simply torturing him, but Willow disagreed. From what she could gather, Tate had closed himself off from moving forward, based on his past. No more family. No more friends. No swimming, even though he was surrounded by the ocean.

And no driving…though her suspicion that he feared going over the ocean bridge leading to the mainland was simply speculation at this point.

She wasn't going to get in the water again. No way would she risk a repeat of her last little wade-in. And forcing him to see her in the water now seemed cruel. But there was no harm being on the sand. He needed to accept that and stop making demands and refusing to talk things out with her like adults.

Somehow she knew she could help Tate break free from the boundaries he'd let his past impose on him—but that meant she had to stay.

Of course, the tension was even higher now than when they'd had sex. And some tiny stubborn part of her refused to tell him she had finally taken the pill. But that was mostly his own fault. Once their last personal conversation was over, he'd retreated back behind the wall of cold professionalism. She knew it was for the best, but it didn't ease any of the heartache she felt.

Her pride—and to an extent, the female part of her that still wanted to be more than just his employee—insisted he had to come to her if he wanted an update.

But all the hyperawareness and tiptoeing around did make dinner with her family tonight a welcome prospect.

By the time early evening came around, Tate didn't stop her from leaving, but again she felt his watching her as she guided her little car down the drive. Her tension faded as she crossed the bridge to the mainland. When she arrived home, she was immediately comforted by the presence of her family. But she also found herself uneasy with all the secrets she was keeping from them.

"It's so wonderful to have everyone back here," Auntie said. "I miss having all of you under one roof."

Jasmine grinned at her as she settled her daughter into her high chair. "You see us almost every day when I drop off Rosie."

"And what am I? Chopped liver?" Ivy asked.

"It's not the same, though," Auntie said before she frowned at Ivy, who was the only one currently living at home, "and you spend all your time at work or in your room."

Ivy's creamy skin flushed when everyone looked her way. "I'm working a lot."

Willow sympathized. "Your boss still out of town?"

Ivy gave a short, stiff nod, but kept silent. Willow made a note to catch up with her younger sister in private.

"How's your job going?" Royce asked.

"Just fine," Willow replied. Maybe too quickly. "A little boring actually."

Jasmine narrowed her eyes, apparently not sold on Willow's lie. "Is Mr. High and Mighty off his high horse yet?" she asked.

"I'm not sure that's possible," Willow answered, giving a silly smile.

Everyone laughed, as she'd planned, but Royce's expression was serious when he added, "As long as you're okay."

She and Jasmine exchanged a look. It felt weird to have a man looking out for them, but in a nice way. "I'm good," she assured them, ignoring the hitch in her voice. Maybe Jasmine would, too, but Willow doubted it.

Later, when Royce took Rosie to the other room to clean her up and change her, Ivy finally opened up. "I have to find a new job."

"What?" Jasmine asked.

"Why?" Willow added at the same time.

Ivy's gaze met theirs in turn, her big beautiful eyes filling with tears. "I'm pregnant."

They each froze for a moment, shocked into silence. Then they all rushed from their various sides of the table to surround her, a wall of feminine comfort that would surely protect Ivy from the outside world.

Auntie was the first to offer a coherent question. "Honey, is that why you've been moping?"

Ivy grimaced. "That and I can't handle the smell of, well, pretty much anything." She glanced at the stove with its half-empty pots and pans.

All of them were aware of how this had come about, so there was no use asking silly questions like who the father was. Willow, sensitive from her own struggles with the man who was her employer, asked, "And he's never said—"

Ivy shook her head. "Not a single word. Every phone conversation since he left has been strictly business. After the first two weeks, I was afraid to bring our… night together…up myself. Now, I'm petrified."

For the first time, Willow was very grateful to Tate. She would not enjoy facing this. Their conversations might have been a strain and not gone in the direction she wanted, but she was glad they'd had at least that much.

"But you can't just walk out," Jasmine insisted. "You're having his baby."

Ivy's look was a little wild-eyed. "Do you seriously think he's up for this after a month and a half of silence? And what about his family? The McLemores are extremely close. There's no way they would accept me." She met each of their gazes in turn. "I've never talked about my family with him—for a reason."

Jasmine and Willow eyed each other for a moment. Willow's heart sank. Grudges lasted a long time in Savannah, especially within the upper classes. Sometimes over stupid, insignificant stuff. After all, rich people could afford to be a little eccentric.

But not this. Never this. Ivy's boss belonged to the family that had run theirs out of town three generations ago. The McLemores. The fact that the Harden sisters' last name was now different due to their grandmother's marriage was the only thing that allowed Ivy to get her executive assistant job for the highly recognized Savannah shipping exec or allowed Jasmine to run an event planning business for Savannah's elite.

No one could immediately connect them with the family wrongfully run out of town after the McLemores' prize ship was torched, with their beloved son inside. But the McLemore family was still run by a matriarch who remembered those days all too well, and the Hardens had to be careful.

Being able to prove that their ancestors weren't responsible for that horrible tragedy would have given them a measure of protection. Willow felt a twinge of guilt over how little progress she'd made in her mission. Her struggles with Tate had taken up her every waking thought lately. The truth about their past would have helped so much in Ivy's current predicament.

Willow and Jasmine had advised Ivy not to take the job in the first place, but she had a deep desire to provide for herself after being taken care of by her sisters for so many years. It had been a huge promotion, and she'd excelled.

It had been well worth the risk—until now.

"You knew who he was. Why did you go home with him?" Jasmine moaned.

Ivy's eyes filled with tears. "I love him."

Willow was sure Jasmine's heart melted just like hers.

"I know—it's stupid and impractical. I thought, in hopelessly optimistic fashion, it would all work itself out." Ivy buried her face in her hands. "I was so naive."

They all were—to think they could mingle with Savannah's elite and never have their past revealed. Jasmine hugged her sister, offering comfort, but Willow was formulating a plan. Her own recent experiences in mind, she asked first and foremost, "Do you want to keep it?"

"Yes." Sincerity showed through Ivy's tears. "I just don't know what to do. If he wanted me, wouldn't he have said so by now?"

"Who knows what men think," Auntie said. Though her one husband was long deceased, she spoke with a note of experience.

Jasmine nodded. "They're supposed to be the less emotional sex, but their actions don't always make logical sense."

All people were influenced by their pasts, as Willow well knew. "The best thing for now is to get you out of that office before he gets back. Don't turn in your resignation yet. Just request time off through HR."

Willow knew Ivy had plenty of vacation time to cover a two-weeks' notice. The important thing was not to alert her boss that she was leaving before absolutely necessary.

She continued, "We'll worry about everything else later. Let me see what I can find at Sabatini House before we make any further decisions." Willow's mission had just turned from interesting to urgent.

"Thank you," Ivy said.

Then Willow saw her sister's normally porcelain skin take on a literal green tinge before she rushed

for the powder room in the hall. Jasmine quickly followed.

Willow watched them go, momentarily grateful she'd
swallowed that little pill.

Nine

Filled with determination after learning of her sister's plight, Willow didn't waste any time in searching Sabatini House further once she got back—only waiting long enough for Tate to get good and settled in his suite.

As she picked her way down the hall, she carefully avoided the areas of the floor she'd learned were creaky in an effort to make as little noise as possible.

The keys she had slid in her pocket when Tate had discovered her earlier now rested in her clasp. But as she approached the door to the third floor, she felt the pull of the nursery once more.

She justified her return by telling herself she could look for clues that she'd missed before—lame as that might be. The dual sets of toys and furniture still fascinated her, but she forced herself past them to the bureaus in the second part of the room. The miniature flashlight she used to get around the house at night helped her find and go through the drawers.

The first bureau held only clothes. The second was more interesting, though not helpful in her mission.

An entire drawer held loose photos of the twins—their mischievous grins and black curls making her heart ache. They all seemed to be professional shots rather than candid photos. And if she guessed right, the woman in the photos when the boys were babies wasn't their mother…she was too young. Maybe a nanny?

Willow slipped one of the pictures of the boys as teens into her pocket without thought.

The next drawer was filled to the brim with books—everything from picture books to Hardy Boys mysteries. Unlike the uniform hardbacks on the shelves, these were mostly paperback, tattered and worn. Had Tate's love of the written word started young? Had it served as an escape for him? For his twin?

A book in one of the right-hand stacks drew her eye. Willow picked it up and flipped through. It looked like a pictorial history of the Kingston family. Obviously handmade. Willow didn't take Tate's parents for artsy-craftsy types. Maybe the nanny had made this?

Unable to resist, Willow sank to the carpet and opened the book properly for a closer look. There weren't pictures in the front, but a story written in graceful, curvy lettering that described a pirate who came to the island, staked his claim and built Sabatini House—just as Tate had said.

It was the whitewashed version, of course. Whoever had written the book to teach the little ones their family history had kept the audience in mind.

Willow could relate. She remembered discovering their own family was descended from pirates. As children, she and her sisters would dress in long, oversize raincoats their mother had bought at the thrift store, tied with sashes, and spend long days pretending to fight with swords and walk the plank.

Their father had relayed stories of how their ancestor had established himself as a good man, stressing the importance of pride and respectability in their family.

Willow's research had born those stories out—theirs was a legacy of integrity for generations. She refused to believe those values had failed enough to allow her great-grandfather to burn down that ship.

But what about Tate's?

When Willow got to the part of the book with the actual photographs of Tate's ancestors, she could actually see some of the qualities he'd mentioned.

She was used to studying historical photos for her own research purposes—personal and professional. The progression of the camera and photo development technology was a familiar concept to her, but these images went beyond simply having to hold still for a long exposure.

Both the men and women were stern-looking, almost

dour in most cases. But it was more about the look in their eyes—the hard way their gazes were trained on the camera. Aggressive, almost forcefully suspicious.

In the group shots, she could see the same manner in the children, who were always held by servants rather than a relative, giving the impression of a hands-off, impersonal form of childrearing.

Willow found herself holding her breath as she turned the pages, hoping to be surprised by a portrait with a more familial casual arrangement. But it never came.

There were only more stiff suits and strong postures and direct stares. Definitely not the friendliest group, even as the cameras had improved over time enough to not require the more somber expressions.

Which left Willow even more curious as to whether those unfeeling looks translated into the ruthless way of life Tate had described.

Had they feuded with the other local shipping barons? Had they settled one of those feuds with death and destruction? Murdoch had hinted that might be the case.

The chime of the grandfather clock in the upper hall jarred her. Time to move on. Willow dropped the book back into the drawer and gathered the flashlight. Back at the door to the third floor, she juggled the flashlight while trying to jiggle the key in the uncooperative lock.

Suddenly she heard a noise.

Unable to place exactly what it was, Willow strained to listen. She quickly flicked off the flashlight. Standing stock-still, she studied the darkness of the hall over her shoulder. She did not want a repeat of the last time.

When nothing happened, she turned back to the door. The decision had barely been made when the sound came again.

This time she could clearly hear a person's voice, though not what they were saying. Fear exploded inside her. A voice in the house could mean only one thing— Tate was awake.

Backtracking, Willow rushed to get back near her room while she listened out for the source, because she had no doubt now that someone was there. No way would she make it to the third floor tonight.

Sure enough, when she reached the door to Tate's suite, she heard a muffled voice. Was he on the phone? Not good.

At least he hadn't caught her first. He wasn't the type to retreat from a confrontation. So what was he doing? Unable to quell her curiosity, she dropped the key and flashlight in her room, then crept back in the dark to stand outside his bedroom door.

She'd barely been there sixty seconds when she clearly heard a shout. She froze. It came again. Was he being attacked?

Willow rushed inside before giving herself time to think. A quick sweep of her gaze over the deep shadows of the room indicated she and Tate were the only ones here. He thrashed on the bed, throwing off his covers as he called out. As she crossed to him, hot memories of the last time she'd been in this room flashed through her brain. She didn't want to remember, didn't want to ache to have Tate's skin against hers once more. But the memories wouldn't completely recede.

She tried to focus on the present instead. The sadness and sympathy brought on by the combination of his earlier description of his parents and the pictures from the book pushed her forward until she could lay her hand on his brow.

He didn't have a fever, but she could feel the tremors that racked him in his sleep. Leaning forward, she started whispering nonsense the way she did to Rosie when she was sick.

It took several minutes, but eventually he began to settle down. He seemed to be sleeping deeply despite the ruckus, so Willow slowly pulled her hand back. Retreating was harder than she'd anticipated. She fought her natural desire to help and her ache to be close to Tate when his guard was down. Still, she forced herself away from him. Back one step. Two.

Just when she thought she'd get away undetected, she found herself grappled into a bear hug that cut off her breath and toppled her to the bed.

The nightmare slowly faded as Tate squeezed down hard on his pillow. Only his pillow felt flesh-firm and warm. The shaking he hadn't experienced in years slowly dissipated as his nostrils filled with a sweet vanilla fragrance. The scent mingled with the heat beneath his cheek. It seemed to surround him, hotter at the base of his neck and along the side of his temple.

He welcomed the invasion of sensation and scent. Anything would be better than reliving his brother's death over and over, but this moment was especially sweet. Somehow he knew that if he could focus on it, then the nightmare would fully recede.

Then he realized his pillow was moving...breathing. *Willow.*

Her presence didn't surprise him. He simply accepted it, welcomed it. He had just enough awareness to ask.

"Willow?"

"It's okay, Tate."

A shudder ran through his body. He clenched his fists as desire washed over him like a wave. In this one thing, he needed to be sure. "You know what I want."

"Yes..." she murmured, "and I'm still here."

Then the forceful surge of need inside his body drowned out all the questions. No thinking. He simply twisted until she lay flat beneath him, then buried his face against her neck.

It was the only bit of bare skin he could find—but it wasn't nearly enough. He nuzzled, eager to taste what smelled so good. He sucked in the vanilla-scented air. Would she let him eat her up?

The way she sunk her fingers into his hair seemed like an invitation. Tentatively he licked her. The taste was even better than he'd imagined. Warm sweetness.

Musky woman. And something he could describe only as life.

He indulged in a slow glide of his tongue from the ridge of her collarbone up to the tip of her chin. His entire body pressed into her as he moved, craving complete contact. Her pulse throbbed beneath his tongue, picking up speed until he lost count of the beats. Her moans filled the air around them.

Never had he felt as alive as he did in this moment. Every stroke of his body against hers was both a relief and fuel for the fire. The blood pounded through him, his body demanding to take what it wanted. She arched into him as if she needed the same.

Tate lost himself in the sensations. He'd never wanted anyone like this before…shouldn't want her now. But logic seemed to have no influence over his body. He wanted her. He would have her.

Again.

Just as he moved to slip his fingers beneath the hem of her shirt, a deluge of emotions and anger washed over him. It was a realization that had propelled him through the last week of living with her. He couldn't take her again. That would be the utmost in stupidity.

But you have a box of condoms. Sure he did. He might have been convinced he would never have sex with Willow again, but he wasn't stupid. He'd bought condoms when he'd bought the pill. No way was he risking impregnating her. If he hadn't already…

His body throbbed hard, as if telling him he should

take her any way he could get her. It was that primal urge to show the world that this woman was his. Only she wasn't. She could never be.

And it wasn't fair to lead her on just so he could satisfy his body's urges.

But this wasn't just about his urges. Her racing pulse wasn't the only clue as to how much she wanted him. Her gasps were enhanced by soft, sweet moans. Her hips lifted to cradle his. Her hands clutched at his forearms, pulling him closer instead of pushing him away.

All he had to do was press his mouth over hers and it would happen. He'd be slow this time, thorough enough to learn every inch of her curvy body. An experience neither of them would forget…

Which was why he forced his body back, pulled his mouth away from that delectable skin. He couldn't do this to himself, and he wouldn't do this to her. Words wouldn't come. He simply rolled to his feet and stood with fists clenched in an effort not to change his mind.

She lay frozen on the bed for a long moment. The only sound in the room was the two of them struggling for air. Was she confused? Afraid to provoke him? Working her way back to sanity right along with him? From the incredible response of her body to his, probably the latter.

Please let it be the latter.

Finally she propped herself up on her elbow. He could sense her gaze, even though he couldn't see more than a faint outline in the darkness of the room. This wasn't like the mainland. There wasn't any ambient light to turn the shadows gray. It was pitch-black, especially when there was only a sliver of moon like tonight.

"Are you okay now?" she asked.

Like the instant a match meets its striker, anger flared. At himself…for caving in to weakness. For letting the nightmare in. At her…for being the very thing he needed. For being the very thing he shouldn't have.

"You shouldn't have come in here," he said, his voice low and gravelly. The desire that burned so close to the surface transformed easily into the aggression he needed to keep himself from taking her. He didn't know how else to burn it off, so he let her be the object of his desire…and his rage.

He wasn't the only one who was angry. She shot up off the bed onto her feet. "I shouldn't have come in here? When I heard you yelling behind a closed door? Excuse me for caring."

"Why would you?" While he said it as a challenge, part of him truly wanted to know. He was fully aware of how callously he treated her. The constant hot and cold. Why would she care about someone like him being in pain?

"I have no idea." Exhaustion seemed to weigh her down. But she tossed one more retort over her shoulder as she made for the door. "Next time I'll just leave you to be strangled in your sleep."

"It would be better than the alternative."

She froze. His eyes had adjusted to the dark enough

that he could see her stop, though he sensed the lack of movement more than anything. Her next words told him everything he couldn't see in her expression. "I didn't realize that being close to me was so repulsive. I'll do my best to help you avoid this situation in the future."

Her deliberate misconstruction of his statement only added fuel to his temper. "That would be helpful," he snarled. "It's all your fault. If you hadn't come here with all your questions and prying and stubbornness…"

He dropped onto the edge of the bed, grateful the pitch-black hid the moisture that welled in his eyes. Still he rubbed his palms against them for good measure. "I miss him. I'd blocked it out for years, remembering only what I had to and now—" he pounded his fist against the mattress "—this. I haven't had this nightmare in forever. Why did you have to come here?"

Despite his accusations, she edged closer. "It shouldn't stay locked away, Tate. He was your brother."

"He was my biggest mistake. Losing him should have marked the end of my life."

"No."

The pressure inside him reached explosive levels. "It has to," he yelled. "I can't live like this. With the memories and emotions and pain. I want to go back to being numb."

"But was that really living?"

Ten

I wonder what kind of mood His Highness is in today.

Willow knew she had an attitude, but it was beyond her to do anything about it. Tate might have finally pushed her past her limits. Either that or she had the worst case of PMS known to the history of womankind.

Still, the man was driving her nuts. As she climbed the stairs to collect the laundry from his dressing room, instances from the last few days played through her mind. Tate had literally skulked like a schoolboy after their last confrontation. Willow would know—she'd dealt with this type of behavior all the time in her freshman classes.

Tate should have grown up by now, but the isolated

lifestyle he'd set up for himself kept him from having to evolve his face-to-face communication skills.

That was only her opinion, of course. Possibly influenced by her bad mood, but still justifiable based on his actions.

Several times each day, she asked herself why she didn't just leave. Or why he didn't send her away. She couldn't speak for him, but she still had things she needed to accomplish here. If she could just find the opportunity... Even though he spent so much time in his office, she was afraid to breach the third floor with him so close. She'd never been the person who got away with things. Somehow, she always ended up getting caught.

She had explored the entirety of the first and second floor rooms, though. Her lack of findings told her that what she really needed, if any evidence remained at all, was hidden in the historical wealth stored on the third floor.

She refused to let her sisters down. Willow had always been one to go the extra mile for others, even if she was too afraid to do something for herself. Maybe that's why she stayed. Having seen the man behind the angry facade, some of the pain and fear Tate carried around with him on a daily basis, Willow didn't feel comfortable simply walking away. Tate needed someone...even if he refused to admit it.

The sound of typing as she walked back past his office distracted her from her gloomy thoughts for a moment. Tate's bad attitude didn't seem to have affected his work. But the fact that she still didn't know what that work entailed only irked her further...

She carried the laundry down into the basement, none too eager to get any of her chores done today. The main drawback to living in was that her job didn't end. And she had a very difficult time justifying spending a couple of hours in bed with a good book when her boss could clearly see she wasn't working.

What she needed was a good night out with her sisters. Margaritas, chips and salsa, and lots of juicy gossip. That sounded like heaven right about now.

Especially after the brief, brittle conversation she'd had with Tate yesterday. She'd been cleaning up after dinner, looking forward to a night spent reading her newest novel once Tate retired to the isolation of his office, when she'd felt him pause behind her in the kitchen.

"Did you take it?"

Willow didn't pretend not to know what he was talking about, even though his question was short to the point of rudeness. He had a right to know.

"Yes."

To her surprise, he went still instead of immediately walking away. She turned to him, feeling that he wanted to say something more. It was an ethereal connection, as if they both wanted to acknowledge what had happened but didn't have the words to reach out to each other.

Then he left.

Willow sorted her loads and got the washing machine started, then shuffled her way back toward the stairs. Enthusiasm for the mundane tasks of her job had completely fled at this point. She couldn't quite figure out a way to resurrect it, except to continue her exploration of the house that had proved to be even more full of surprises than she'd anticipated. It just refused to give her the one piece of information she, and Ivy, desperately needed right now.

As she paused beside the door to the mythical underground cave—she refused to believe it was actually real until Tate let her see it in person—Willow leaned against the door and tried to let go of the unusual exhaustion that plagued her. The sound of the rushing waves soothed her. A swim would be nice, but she couldn't bring herself to do that to Tate right now.

Despite her current irritation.

As much as she resented his attitude the other night, she realized a lot of it was born of pain. He'd settled into a cocooned way of life that allowed him to keep the memories and emotions at bay. Until she'd started digging all that stuff out, dragging it into the open and forcing him to acknowledge it once more. That couldn't be comfortable. Some days she wondered if it was even safe. If she'd opened a Pandora's box she should have left alone.

But there wasn't anyone here to give her an answer to that. So she had to make her best guesstimate and move on. As much as she might resent his attitude, knowing where it came from made her want to stay, to see whatever this was through to the end.

She'd never been a quitter just because things got difficult.

Opening her eyes after long minutes of simply standing, breathing and listening to the waves, Willow was surprised to see a door toward the far end of the corridor that she'd never noticed before. Not all the way on the end, which she would have seen each time she entered the hallway. This was a slim door about three-quarters of the way down that occupied a shadowy area, in contrast to a bright patch of sunlight let in by the window right before it.

Sabatini House was full of all kinds of cool nooks and crannies. She'd found odd closets, weirdly shaped rooms and all kinds of architectural goodies that either came original to the house or had been modernized over the last few generations. So as she walked down the hallway, excitement lightened her step for just a moment. Even if it was just an empty room with a couple of spiderwebs, it would be interesting to see and speculate on its use.

Except, as she should have come to expect by now, the door was locked. She knew where the downstairs keys were and had never been officially told these rooms were off-limits. She huffed a little laugh as she ran upstairs to the utility room for the keys. She ran back down and in no time was turning the handle to get inside.

At first glance, the little room served as straight storage. Slightly larger than a walk-in closet, it was over three-quarters full of plain brown boxes, all uniform in size. That, in and of itself, struck her as odd. The house had a few rooms that housed old furniture and odds and ends. Her glimpse into the third floor had shown lots of trunks and cabinets and such. Even the nursery's contents were either covered with tarps or stored inside drawers.

But so far she hadn't seen uniform packing boxes like this anywhere else in the house.

So what made the contents of these so special? Taking a few steps closer, she could see that some had the tape broken on the top, but most of them had never been opened. Definitely odd. Willow reached for the nearest open box and pulled back the flaps.

Granted, the one lighting fixture in the small room didn't do a fantastic job, but even then she wasn't sure she was trusting her eyesight. Because all she could see was books.

Actually, multiple copies of the same book. *The Secret Child* by Adam Tate.

Willow wasn't sure how long she stood staring, trying to resolve what she was seeing with the truth it had to represent. No one was enough of a fan to have twenty-five copies of the same book. Publishers had those…and authors.

How could he have kept this a secret from her?

Just to make sure, she sped from box to box, check-

ing to see that they were all the same. *The Red Light.
The Encroaching Sea. The Third Floor.* All Adam Tate
books. And with each title she read, excitement and
irritation grew inside her. Finally she ran out into the
hall, leaving the door open behind her. She rushed up
the stairs and down the passage until she reached Tate's
office door.

She felt vaguely surprised that the door wasn't
locked, but couldn't stop long enough to analyze why
that might be. Bursting through, she ran in a few steps
before skidding to a stop before his large black desk.
Tate stared at her in shock, mouth open, eyes wide.
The same emotions echoed in her own mind, but she
couldn't focus on him. Behind the desk were gorgeous
floor-to-ceiling bookshelves that covered the entire
wall. Light from the large, arched windows shone across
the beloved titles that took front-and-center stage. If she
wasn't mistaken, the shelves contained every Adam Tate
title ever written, along with many other books by her
favorite authors, what looked like nonfiction research
books and several rows of white binders.

Her gaze swept across all of it in an instant, then
back to the man who looked like he was still trying to
process her presence.

"You jerk. Why wouldn't you tell me that you're
Adam Tate?"

In shock, Tate reverted to his natural response.
"What are you doing in my office?"

"Answer my question."

Her hands-on-hips stance did not bode well for brushing her off. "Willow—"

"We aren't talking about just any author here. You knew how I felt about those stories. You talked to me about his—your—books and just decided that it wasn't worth mentioning that you wrote them? Seriously?"

Frustration tightened Tate's muscles. Shutting down his computer screen, he shoved back his chair to pace around the room, pulling at hair that was way past the need for a haircut.

The sudden breeze reminded him of his open button-down shirt. He glanced at Willow, only to see her force her gaze from his abs back to the books.

"Tate, this is incredible," she said, waving her hand at the overflowing shelves. "Why would you keep this a secret?"

That had him raising a brow. "I'm a little bit of a privacy nut."

Her expression told him she was fully aware of that.

"Look, I'm not even sure how people found out I was an author. I never wanted it to be known. Making up stories is my escape. I don't want the recognition."

Willow shook her head. "But…you're Adam Tate. I'm a fan. I live here. Why keep this a secret from *me*? I mean, you know I'm not gonna turn into a creepy stalker, right?"

Looking up, he realized the true issues underlying

this conversation. The point was not his secrecy, nor secrecy in general. The point was how he viewed her.

Tate had given her mixed signals since she first came to Sabatini House. A lot of them were twisted up in his own idiosyncrasies, as he fought against all the things she made him feel. She deserved better than that.

Now that he was truly looking, he could see the hurt dulling those gorgeous green eyes. It shouldn't be there. He'd done his best to keep her at arm's length, but pulling her close was too damn tempting…and he was too damn weak.

They'd shared too much, more than he ever had with anyone else.

Oh, he and Murdoch talked, but unless they were both drunk the conversations were at best on the surface—just the way men liked it. The few serious discussions he could remember involved his parents' deaths and Tate's decision to clear out their stuff.

He and his editor were friendly, would have a meal together outside the office when Tate was in New York, but the conversation was either business or story, which they could discuss for days on end without tiring of the subjects. That was the way book nerds were. That was their bond. Neither of them attempted to bridge that gap, because that was how Tate wanted it.

But with Willow? They'd gone deeply personal. Fast. He'd not only shared his body with her, but his nightmares, his brother, his fears.

Now this.

As he watched her, there was no getting around the stubborn set to that tiny pointed chin, or the determined look in her eyes. He'd learned that much by now. He might as well fess up. Otherwise she'd find a way to drag it out of him.

That might not be pretty for either of them.

"Honestly, I'd never told anyone before. I very rarely meet new people who are interested in discussing what I do for a living. I'm not even sure how to bring it up."

And that was the God's honest truth.

Willow cocked her head to the side. "Well, it's time you got some practice."

Tate almost laughed. Leave it to Willow to be practical rather than sentimental.

"You're not a typical sympathetic kind of girl, are you?"

Willow shrugged, but lowered her lashes as she tried to hide her reaction. Tate had a feeling he'd hit a nerve.

"I feel just as much sympathy as anyone else," she said softly. "But sometimes that isn't what the situation calls for. I grew up in a house full of women. There's always been enough emotion to drown us all in it. Somebody has to be practical if we're gonna actually get moving."

Why did that attitude frustrate him while making him want to kiss her at the same time?

Tate was more than aware that she challenged him, was moving him away from his comfortable status quo to a new level. He shouldn't like her—should push her far away. Fire her, even.

So why was he still aching to do the opposite?

He watched as she circled the desk, her body moving with unconscious sensual grace that hit him right in the gut. It took everything in him to keep from reaching out.

Her long, delicate fingers stroked over the books' spines. "So who did you base the woman on in *The Train*? She was seriously creepy," Willow asked.

"No one," he answered automatically. "She's made up, though the story idea came from an article I read."

"Cool. About what?"

The conversation started just like that. Tate was honestly amazed at how easy it was to suddenly talk about his work. He'd never done it with anyone but his agent and editor before today. Why didn't he resent her intrusion? Rebuff her questions?

Because the whole thing fascinated him. He had to admit, her observations were insightful. Even as they moved on from his books to others on the shelf, Willow brought up points about the stories he'd never even thought of before today. Her brain worked in fascinating ways.

And that was how Tate found himself falling in love with the woman he should never want.

Before he had time to absorb the realization and panic, the house phone rang. Tate gratefully crossed to answer it.

"Hey there, young man," a familiar voice said. "How's today treating you?"

Murdoch's standard greeting was never more welcome. The familiar words had kept Tate grounded and focused on the present for years. Tate needed them now more than ever. "Good as always. And you?"

Tate's ears tuned in to Murdoch's tales of meeting his daughter as an adult, the new grandbaby and this whole new family he had found, but Tate's gaze couldn't be torn away from Willow, who took the liberty to explore his office while he was distracted. He should stop her from invading this last vestige of private space left to him, but her expressive face and the way she reached out to touch everything captured his imagination.

So much so that he lost the flow of the conversation. "I'm sorry, Murdoch. What did you say?" he asked, trying to catch up.

"I said, I hate to do this, boy, but I'm not coming back."

Eleven

Willow wasn't sure what the sound was that caught her attention, but she turned back from the window in the office to find Tate white-knuckling the phone. His normal olive skin was pale beneath the color. Willow had the distinct impression that his sheer will was the only thing keeping him upright.

She took a tentative step toward him. Then another. Tate wouldn't want sympathy, but she had the urge to hug him, just the same.

What was wrong?

When his eyes opened, even they seemed paler versions of themselves. He held out the phone.

"Murdoch wants to talk to you."

Though eager to catch up with her friend, Willow

couldn't forget Tate's look, even after he turned away. With no answers from that corner, she jumped into the conversation headfirst.

"What's wrong?" she asked Murdoch.

A long sigh met her over the airwaves. "I'm sorry, Willow. I'd hoped this would be easier, but I couldn't wait much longer to tell him."

"Tell him what?" Willow's heart pounded in her ears while she waited for his answer.

"I'm not returning. My place is here, with the family I've finally found."

There was a long pause as Willow tried to muster a response. In the background of the call she heard the faint sound of a baby starting to cry.

"I have no idea how much time I have left, so I need as much time with them now as I can get," Murdoch continued. "I let my daughter down. I won't do it again…to her or the little one."

Willow certainly understood. From the first day she'd met him, she'd sensed the utter loneliness inside Murdoch. Finding out he had family out there, especially a daughter starting a family of her own, wasn't something he would turn his back on. She should have realized that as soon as he'd offered her this job.

"I know this is a shock to Tate, but I have to do it," Murdoch said.

At the mention of his name, Willow turned to see how Tate was doing, only to find herself alone in the room.

"Oh, Murdoch. What is he going to do?" She sighed,

free to ask anything now that she was alone. That didn't stop her from worrying.

"I know this will be hard," Murdoch admitted. "But I've devoted my life to the Kingston family. Tate, in particular. He's the only one of them who deserved it, in my opinion." He paused, sighing. "But it's time to devote myself elsewhere, Willow."

She could sense he was trying to convince himself as much as he was her. Bless his heart. "I understand that, Murdoch. It's what you need to do…what you should do. It will just be hard here."

"I was hoping having you there would make it easier."

Huh? "By giving me a summer job?"

"Is it just a summer job?"

Willow could hardly wrap her brain around what he was saying, but was actually surprised she hadn't suspected this before. After all, Murdoch could have easily hired a man for this position, since he knew all of Tate's issues firsthand.

"Murdoch, did you set me up?"

"Not you so much as Tate."

"You could have at least given a girl some warning." So Murdoch had had this in mind all along. Had he known the difficulties it would cause both of them when he'd played matchmaker? She wanted to ask if he was aware Tate didn't keep condoms on hand…but even she didn't have the gall to say that.

"Willow, you're the smartest, most insightful woman

I know. Granted, I don't know many, but sometimes you just know things about a person. I knew without a doubt that if anyone could break Tate out of his self-imposed prison, it would be a woman like you." Silence filtered down the line for a moment. The baby wasn't crying anymore. "He needs you," Murdoch finally said.

No joke. Willow had known that from the beginning, though she hadn't been prepared for what breaking him out of his shell would entail. "But that doesn't mean he's ready for it, Murdoch."

"Or that it will be easy," he agreed. "I'm fully aware that Tate has some unhealthy boundaries in place. Hell, I stood to the side while he planted the line and dug in deep. But he needs to let go. You can do that for him, Willow."

"No, I can't. Only Tate can make those changes for himself."

Murdoch wasn't budging an inch. "But he never will with no one to challenge him."

That got her ruff up a bit. "So you sent me here because you thought I would be difficult to live with?"

"In your own way." He chuckled. "Tell me you haven't shaken things up already."

"More than you know," she mumbled before she thought about the implications of letting that out into the open.

Murdoch grew silent for a long moment. She could almost hear him thinking, but she was afraid of saying anything further. Afraid of bringing her fears to life.

After all, Tate wasn't the only one who was scared of something.

"Then I only have one question," he finally said.

"What's that?"

"Are you okay?"

No. She thought back over all the strange symptoms she'd had since taking the morning-after pill, all the ups and downs of her interactions with Tate, and her own fears about what Murdoch was telling her. She wasn't ready, was she?

"I'm really not sure."

"I'll tell you the two things I've learned since coming here, Willow." His voice was a deep mixture of happiness and regret. "One, love can make even the most fearful thing worthwhile. And two, nothing will ever make loving someone completely easy. You might never be ready…but you've got to take the leap sometime."

Tate sensed Willow's presence even before he heard her. He wanted to go to her, take her, but too much had happened. There was too much to process. Every inch of him, mind and body, felt oversensitized.

"It's not a good idea to be here," he said, wincing at the density in his voice.

He didn't want to scare her off, but the river of emotions and need bubbling up inside him were too deep not to find their way to the surface. Especially in the room that held such sexy memories of her. Where her scent still lingered on the pillow. His imagination could paint the perfect picture of her laid out on his bed in the heat of the afternoon sun.

She needed to stay far away from him.

But she didn't heed his silent warning. Instead she moved closer. "Murdoch needs to be with his family right now, Tate."

He waved off her words with a rough gesture. "I know that! I'm not a selfish teenager anymore, expecting someone to cater to my wants and needs."

If anything, her voice softened further. "That doesn't mean change isn't hard. That it doesn't spark resentment."

In the mirror, he saw her sink onto the edge of his bed. The sight of her vibrant beauty against the navy comforter drew his eye. But he refused to turn, knowing he'd do something rash.

"You know, Tate—" she said, tilting her head to the side. A wash of auburn hair swung into view. "I lost both of my parents when I was a teenager."

Shock froze Tate's entire body for several seconds. "You did?"

She nodded. "Both of them. Car accident."

Though she'd talked about going home for family dinners, Tate had never asked her whom she met with or any of the details. Normally functioning families weren't something he could relate to...in fact, very few of the characters in his books had them. He was more likely to kill off any close relatives or orphan the characters in some way. That isolated lifestyle was one he knew far more about than being part of a happy family.

"Congratulations on turning out far more normal than me," he said, only a touch of bitterness tainting his reply.

"Unlike you, I had a very loving family left even after they were gone. I have two sisters—one older, one younger. My little sister was still young enough to need extra care. We came back to Savannah to live with Auntie."

He shouldn't want to know, but he asked anyway. "Who is she?"

"Not a blood relative at all, actually. Auntie was my grandmother's best friend, and nanny to my mother when she was little. Though she'd moved back to Savannah, they remained close. She adopted all three of us girls and raised us like her own family, even though she'd never been able to have children of her own.

"So losing people I loved was a lot different for me than it was for you. None of that made it easy, just bearable. But if I had my sisters ripped away now, I don't know that I'd survive. They are my support system. I can't imagine losing them."

Tate's voice was raspy as he struggled to speak from tightening lungs. "What will I do?"

"I don't honestly know, but we'll figure it out."

Tate sensed her approach behind him and inhaled at the press of her body against his back, as if she were bracing him for the changes ahead. "Murdoch has been your family, even more than your blood family, for many years. It's okay to grieve," she said.

It had been one thing to have Murdoch leave for a while, hard to accept but doable. To know he wouldn't be coming back, would no longer be part of Tate's daily life… That was something for which Tate was completely unprepared.

Closing his eyes, Tate breathed deep and soaked in the heat of her against him. Oh so slowly, her arms moved up his sides to anchor her against his shoulders. Almost as if they were one, braced against the world. As much as he shouldn't want it, he couldn't turn away from the incredible feeling of her melding with him.

When the need grew too strong, he moved toward her instead. Chest-to-chest. Face-to-face. He buried his hands in that fiery hair. He had to have her, had to savor this incredible woman who had come into his life so unexpectedly.

Having made the decision, Tate refused to hurry. If this was the only taste of heaven he ever had, he wouldn't rush it.

Using his hands to tilt her head back, he traced her lips with his tongue. Memorizing every part of her became his top priority, no matter how loudly his body demanded he take her right now.

Her perfectly full lips had a slightly salty taste. He couldn't hold back a groan as he pushed deeper. So hot. So responsive. Her tongue reached to meet his. Something about holding her like this, demanding entry and receiving her surrender, spiked his pleasure. He massaged her scalp. Her neck muscles loosened, her head falling back into his palms. Knowing he brought her pleasure, too, made his head spin.

He could barely move far enough away to pull her shirt over her head. The sight of the soft upper curves of her breasts in the dappled light made his muscles tighten. He could almost stand there looking all night. Cupping them in his hands, he squeezed lightly. Her breath caught. The material of her bra was thin enough for him to feel her nipples peak against his palms. Rubbing across them in short circles had them both moaning. She swayed. Willow's hands returned to his biceps, her fingers pressing into him in search of stability.

He loved that his touch made her body go weak.

How much longer they could both stand, he wasn't sure. Quickly he lifted her, then laid her out on the bed like a feast for his senses. Gorgeous pale skin. Sweet vanilla scent. Fresh, vibrant taste. And hot, burning touch. What had he ever done to deserve such a precious gift?

He removed each piece of clothing with exquisite care. He pulled her shorts down over long, shapely legs. Panties followed the same path, revealing the neat patch of red hair that protected her most delicate skin. She arched so he could unhook her bra, allowing him to see the dark pink nipples he'd so insistently aroused.

His own clothes came off with more speed and efficiency. Even though he was in danger of being carried away by his passion for her, Tate didn't forget to reach into his bedside table for a condom. This time he would protect *her*, even more than he'd tried to protect himself.

Her body welcomed him eagerly. Tate gasped as her muscles made way for him, bathing him in her liquid heat. He squeezed his eyes shut. Somewhere deep inside, he found the control that kept him from pounding into her. From finishing before they'd both milked every ounce of pleasure from this moment.

Instead he thrust lightly into her, relishing every lift of her hips for more. The feel of her nails scraping down his chest jolted him closer to the edge. He bent low, licking and sucking at the delicate skin of her neck, feeling her cries against his lips. When she squeezed those supple legs around his hips, he could hold back no longer.

Now thrusting hard, Tate drove them both higher, seeking that ultimate explosion. For the first time, he felt as though they were seeking together with a need that transcended physical release. Somehow he knew this moment with Willow was a unique promise…a bond that would never be broken.

Twelve

Willow rolled over on her back, sure something wasn't right. It took her a moment to realize that she wasn't in her own bed. And another moment to realize that she was alone in Tate's.

While she was trying to banish the fog from her brain, she heard the rare sound of the plane as it gained altitude, climbing away from the island. Despite the gray darkness before dawn, Tate was already on his way.

Willow tried not to be hurt but found it hard to keep her emotions on an even keel. Yesterday and last night had been incredible. Though she tried to remind herself that Tate was probably just reaching out for human contact after learning about Murdoch, that didn't mean he had to take off without telling her. But the very fact she felt that way told her everything she needed to know about herself in this situation—as much as she might try to be a modern woman taking things one day at a time, she was really more of a relationship kind of girl.

Which meant in the end, she was probably going to end up hurt.

She padded downstairs in Tate's shirt, because she could. As she reached for the coffeepot, she found his note.

Wasn't sure you remembered. I have a meeting with Charles today. See you later tonight.

Oh, right. Willow laughed a little, glad Tate hadn't been here when she overreacted. Now she felt a little silly getting upset over something he'd already told her about. He was meeting with his editor to discuss the first book on the new contract today.

But things were always unsettled with Tate. One minute off; one minute on. No wonder she jumped to conclusions.

Staring out the window, she inhaled deeply. The dark, smooth scent of coffee filled the air. She took a couple more breaths, searching for calm. Rain started to sprinkle outside the window. They were supposed to have some showers, then a couple of overcast days before a major storm came ashore. She'd hoped to swim while Tate wasn't here to hover, but she didn't want to risk it in the rain.

Then again, she knew what she could do…

She smiled as she poured herself a cup, then added a substantial amount of cream. Just the way she liked it. That first sip was always heavenly, but today it made her frown.

After a minute, she tried again. Ugh. Her creamer must have gone sour. She'd get some more tomorrow. With the storm developing, Willow wanted to make sure they had everything they needed to be off the grid for a few days. Also, lunch with her sisters was always a plus.

Eager to do what she'd put off too many times already, Willow changed her clothes, then headed to the door to the third floor at the far end of the hall. She worked the key in the door, finally getting the tough lock to turn. The stairs beyond were crusted along the edges with thick dust, but the centers were clean from the recent treks of the workmen who made the repairs.

The first couple of rooms were disappointingly empty. Another one had an empty bed frame and a chifforobe filled with women's formal clothes that could date back to the twenties and thirties.

Then—jackpot.

The door was still open to the room directly over hers, giving her a clear view of the trunks and rolltop desk she'd seen that night. It felt like forever since she'd watched the ceiling fall down on her that first night. So much had happened since then.

A quick peek showed the room across was almost identical, but even more loaded with stuff. It would be hard to walk in there without tripping over something.

Goodness, there were enough storage trunks that she could be here all day. After a good look around, she started with the first room because everything had been carefully moved to one side during the work, making it tidier. Maybe that would make it easier to search through.

But the more she looked, she realized the dates on the papers in the boxes and trunks were too current to be relevant. For what she was looking for anyway. Unfortunately, as a history buff, all of it was interesting, so she was slow in making her way through the materials.

Finally she moved to the next room. When she was barely halfway across a loud boom shook the house. Willow jumped. A shaky laugh escaped her. The shutters were all closed, so she hadn't realized a bigger storm had moved in. Rain, too. The drops suddenly came down heavy and hard on the roof. She hoped Tate had been able to fly clear of it.

Now to the task at hand.

The thick layer of dust in this room suggested it had been untouched for years, possibly decades. Fortunately, everything was neatly boxed. Unfortunately, there weren't any labels to give her a preview of what was in each trunk…and they weren't all easy to open.

She could sure use a handy crowbar right about now.

Practical planner that she was, she started at the wall by the door and worked her way around. Before long, crouching had her thighs screaming in pain, so she just plopped herself down on the dusty hardwood floor.

The first thing to slow her down was that she didn't know exactly what she was looking for. She wanted proof that exonerated her family, but didn't know what form said proof would take. That meant looking at a lot of pieces of paper so she didn't miss anything.

But the dates on the documents were close to the period when the crime took place—if she could just find the exact year. That much, at least, she knew.

Tate's family hadn't been big on personal accounts, it seemed, but they were big on business. There were no diaries or cards or letters but lots of ledgers and files and dust. Eventually she seemed to hit the sweet spot—a trunk of dated ledgers. At one time it seemed to have been padlocked, but someone had unlocked it and simply slipped the lock back into place without forcing it closed.

Bingo! There was the year she needed.

Only a few pages in she realized Tate had been telling the honest truth about his relatives. His ancestor, Joseph Kingston, had been a bad, bad boy.

These weren't your typical business ledgers—they contained everything that couldn't be kept with the "official" records.

According to the neatly written pages, repeated payment went to the same four or five individuals throughout the year in question. Probably local troublemakers, if Willow had to guess. Though the entries didn't list exactly what the men were hired for—which was a big warning sign in Willow's brain—they did list locations, times, special supplies needed and either a company or family name.

Willow's heart pounded over both the historical and personal significance of what she was reading. Joseph Kingston had systematically waged war on others in their regional community. Not a week went by without an entry.

How much property damage did this thick ledger represent? And how many lives were lost when people carelessly got in the way?

Like the McLemores' heir.

Willow wondered if she could link these dates to incidents reported in the local newspapers at the time. The researcher in her was excited. Quickly she flipped through to the date she most needed.

There was an entry. She scanned through and found the memo line—McLemore.

For a few seconds, Willow savored the elation of discovery. This could make a big difference for her sister—just the confidence of being able to cast doubt if Paxton McLemore's family accused her of anything was huge. Now they would be prepared for the conflict they all knew was coming.

But what about Tate?

For the first time, Willow thought about him in all of this. As she carried the ledger downstairs to her room, she thought over all that he'd been through lately. As private as he was, how would he feel about this part of his family history becoming known?

* * *

As Tate let himself into Sabatini House after mid-night, he was curious in what state he would find Willow. Though they'd both known he'd be gone today, he was pretty sure she would have forgotten by morning—hence the note he'd left. He'd been trying to keep himself out of the doghouse, so why had he still felt like he was bailing when he let himself out before dawn?

As Tate walked through the empty, dimly lit kitchen, he was at least grateful she didn't jump out and start lecturing him…though his mind's picture of Willow in full-on irate-professor mode was pretty entertaining. Realizing the lower levels of the house were quiet, he climbed the stairs, his body growing hard at the question of whether she would be in his bed.

He didn't have the right to demand it. He didn't even know if she thought she belonged there. After all, he'd never given her reason to believe it was where he wanted her all the time. He only knew the ache for her had been constant all day, but now it ramped up to screaming level.

He shouldn't be so greedy, but his body was tired and his psyche was stressed. He wanted the balm he knew Willow could grant him. Besides, he knew what the next few days held, on top of the roller-coaster ride of the last few.

Which brought him full circle. Would she want him again? Or would she want him nowhere near her?

Nerves ate him up as he rounded the corner for the

hall to his suite…and hers. Willow had slept every night since the first in her bed with the door closed. Part of him was resigned to finding his access cut off by the door to her room. Instead his gaze was drawn to a square of light on the floor.

Her door was open. The light was on. Tate set his briefcase and carry bag against the wall, then unbuttoned his shirt as he strode toward her door.

She lay curled away from him facing the lamp that put out soft light on the bedside table. Eager to see her, he moved to the end of the bed with soft steps. One of her hands cradled her cheek as she slept. The other rested over one of his paperback books, as if she'd fallen asleep reading.

The softest of feelings wrapped around Tate's chest like a thick, plush blanket. It wasn't the same as the spark of passion or the sting of regret. Nor the heat of anger.

Softness had never had a place in his life. What little he'd experienced he'd had no use for. So why did he embrace whatever was happening now?

He had no answers but was grateful when the warm glow was swept away by a heated wave of passion. This he was familiar with. This he could handle.

Not soon enough he was stripped to his boxers and slipping into the bed beside her. Every time he was with Willow brought new experiences to him, new insights. But tonight, of all the things he remembered, that first moment when she opened her eyes and smiled sleepily at him hit him square in the chest and stayed with him to the next day.

Her gorgeous welcome allowed him to fall asleep, but the unfamiliar bed and all-too-familiar thoughts pushed him from her way too early. He didn't sleep well at the best of times, but this time of year it was impossible for him to get more than a few hours at a time. Thoughts of his brother, of his guilt, made rest illusive.

Like a beacon, the water lured Tate downstairs, past his forgotten briefcase and carry-on and the coffee he needed to start each day. All the way to the door he opened only once a year. It had started calling a few days early this year.

Tate stood for long time with his palm pressed against the door that led to the underground swimming cave, as if testing the temperature. This was the place his family had seen as a symbol of their life force. They had started on the water. Made their home on the water. Made their living on the water. They'd had enough hubris to believe they controlled it.

Tate had learned better.

He forced himself to grasp the handle and turn it. When the door opened, the sound of rushing water filled his ears.

What so many had called an amazing creation didn't inspire awe in him. The dim break of dawn spilled into the deep, low room from the mouth of the cave, allowing him to watch the push and pull of the waves against rocky surfaces long worn smooth. It was not magical.

Not to him. Tate considered the place evil incarnate. The source of his family's power…and with his brother Adam's death, it had become the source of their demise.

Never again would Tate trust the water. It might have been the source of his family's successes, but they'd failed to acknowledge its power to destroy. Now, when he looked at the beach and the waves, or even considered driving across the bridge to the mainland, all he could see was the deceptive calm that hid the malevolent power beneath the surface.

He hated the weakness that came with the fear, but the power was real…and far from benevolent. Tate gripped the door frame hard enough for his hands to ache. He needed the strain to keep him anchored.

Suddenly a delicate hand covered his, a lithe body pressed against his back. Willow didn't try to peek around him. Didn't ask any questions. Instead she rested her cheek between his shoulder blades to once again offer him comfort.

His body shuddered as the tension flowed from him. Her gentle touch reminded him that he wasn't alone.

"Are you okay?" she finally whispered against his bare back.

He wasn't. But for once, with her, that wasn't an insurmountable problem. So he told her the memory that kept him from sleeping in her bed. "Tomorrow would have been his birthday."

Thirteen

Tate's words haunted Willow as she headed to town for supplies. He would spend the day prepping the house for the incoming storm. She'd make sure they had everything they needed—along with a little extra.

That attitude felt a little too close to homemaking for her comfort. Less like a job and more like a desire to take care of someone on a personal level. She tried not to think of it that way, but the association lingered around the edges of her consciousness anyway.

If she could get up the nerve, she planned to throw Tate a little well-deserved celebration. He'd been pleased that his contract negotiations had gone through and had asked her to get something for a special meal, but she was more interested in celebrating his personal milestone than the professional one.

Hopefully he'd enjoy it. From what she'd learned from Murdoch, no one had celebrated Tate's birthday for a long time. Not since his brother's death. Which was beyond sad. She knew he loved his brother, but Tate's life hadn't ended. The fact that his parents had acted as though it had was beyond cruel.

Now she could see how it played out in so many ways in Tate's life. But to her, this one was significant. Letting someone know they were special, that their presence here on earth was appreciated and welcomed, was important to the building of self-worth.

Tate's family got a big fat F for failure in many areas, but especially this one in particular.

Besides, spending some time together, showing him how much she appreciated him as a person, might soften the blow she could feel approaching. As much as she wanted to deny it, she was terribly afraid that his nightmare was about to come true. Her odd symptoms were getting too frequent to ignore.

With that in mind, she turned to her sister Jasmine as they walked together down the aisle at the large, local shopping center. "How is Ivy?"

"Bless her heart, she's miserable," Jasmine said, shaking her head. "The nausea is just killing her. And I don't see how she's going to look for work every day, she's so tired."

"Poor thing," Willow added, but she was turning

the information over in her mind as she pushed the cart down the aisle.

"She's a nervous wreck, too," Jasmine added, oblivious to Willow's distraction. "She only left work a few days ago using her leave, and the replacement keeps calling her, telling her the boss is asking more and more questions."

Willow imagined he was…after all, he knew more than anyone that there was unfinished business between himself and his executive assistant. "She should quit answering the phone."

"That's what I told her. She's putting in all these applications because she insists she should support herself." Jasmine rolled her eyes.

"She's been that way since her first job, you know that. It's a hang-up." They all had them in some form or another.

"Yeah, but she's struggling. I think maybe a job would help her feel like she has some control in this situation. But I really wish she'd give herself a break. I think she's afraid if she waits too long, it will be harder to get work because she'll be closer to term."

Willow shook her head, but she completely understood Ivy's concerns. An employer would have to really want to hire her to overlook a large pregnant belly at an interview.

Getting back to her own worries, Willow asked, "So she's tired and nauseous?" Willow had only one of those symptoms. Did that mean she'd dodged a bullet? Were the other things she'd experienced just an odd coincidence?

"What's that look on your face?"

Willow brought her attention back to Jasmine. *Uh-oh*. Her sister had stopped midaisle to study her...a little too closely. She tried to blank her expression. "What do you mean?"

Jasmine's gaze narrowed. "Don't try that innocent look on me. That hasn't worked with me since you were a little kid with gangly legs."

This was her sister. Willow knew she could trust Jasmine to keep her secrets. It was just—the thought of saying her suspicions out loud scared her. Heck, whispering them even... But Willow really needed someone to talk to.

This wasn't a subject she'd paid any attention to over the years. She could have looked it up, but until now she'd been afraid of confirming that her suspicions were true. And besides, the last thing she wanted filling her brain were all the horror stories floating around the internet.

So Jasmine was her best option.

Willow tried for her most matter-of-fact tone. "What exactly are the symptoms of pregnancy? Besides nausea, of course."

Jasmine gasped, her voice notching up an octave. "Girl! Are you—"

"Would you hush?" Willow demanded, glancing around. It would be just her luck to run into a student while her sister was grilling her about the consequences of her sex life.

Jasmine frowned, but lowered her voice. "What are you trying to say, Willow?"

"Nothing," Willow said, feeling contrary. "I'm trying to ask something, in a subtle way."

"I don't think it worked."

"I noticed."

They stood there staring at each other in stalemate until they both began to giggle… Jasmine was the first to sober up. "So I'm guessing you have reason to believe you might be pregnant?"

"I shouldn't be."

Jasmine simply raised her brows at that. How did she look so elegant all the time, even when she was in interrogation mode? "Would you stop beating around the bush and tell me what's going on?"

Willow lowered her voice even more. "I took a morning-after pill, so I thought everything would be okay. But I've felt weird ever since."

Jasmine's frown echoed her own.

"But I'm not nauseous. So that's good, right? I'm just exhausted. And things taste weird. And sometimes I feel dizzy—"

Jasmine started walking. Willow stared for a few seconds, then hurried to follow. "Where are we going?" she asked.

"For someone who is so smart, you can be incredibly dumb at times," Jasmine said over her shoulder.

Willow should be offended, but she knew her sister was teasing her. "What did I miss?"

Jasmine marched determinedly through the store, leaving Willow confused and a little out of breath as she tried to follow with her full shopping cart. Seeing Jasmine pause to scan the pharmacy section gave her concern, though.

"You do realize that the morning-after pill has a failure rate, right?" Jasmine disappeared down one aisle, then came back with a small box. "Just use this. Then you'll know for sure."

Willow stared down at the pregnancy test, almost afraid to touch it. Then came the nausea…right on schedule.

"Come on," Jasmine urged, nudging the box in her direction. "We can buy it right now and have answers in less than three minutes."

"No," Willow said, appalled at the idea. "I'm not doing that here."

Jasmine's small smile infuriated her. "At the house, then," she countered.

"I'll…" Willow swallowed hard. "I'll take it with me. Then we'll see."

Jasmine quickly snatched the box out of her reach. "As long as you promise to call me when it's done," she insisted.

"Oh, trust me. I'll let you know."

"ASAP. After telling the father, of course."

Now, didn't that sound like a pleasant prospect?

* * *

Tate squeezed his fingers into fists, forcing himself to ignore the ache that told him to continue writing. He'd been in the flow for several hours now. As much as he wanted to continue working, he needed to attend to other matters.

Still, it felt strange for writing to not be the most important thing in his life anymore.

But the clock told him that Willow would be starting dinner about now. They'd talked about something special to celebrate his new contract, but Tate had a few ideas of his own that he hadn't shared. So he saved his document and shut down his computer before heading down the stairs.

As he walked by, he could hear Willow in the kitchen. He smiled. She didn't give herself props for how good of a cook she was. Tate looked forward to every meal, and often came down early for a glimpse of the menu items. But today he kept moving until he reached the front formal living room.

The furniture in this room was from the early sixties, as far as he could tell. He'd never bothered to change it out, because the space wasn't in use. If a family lived here, the large area would be perfect for a leather sectional, a couple of recliners, a large television and maybe a game area, but for just Tate and Murdoch, all that wasn't necessary. He walked through, noting the clean floors and lack of dust. Willow had obviously cleaned the room, even though no one was ever in here.

His steps gradually slowed as he approached the opposite wall. He slowly pulled back the floor-to-ceiling curtains to reveal French doors leading out onto a covered deck. The outdoor space had been used for parties and long summer days by the ocean.

At least, it had been by his parents.

Tate hadn't set foot out here since they died. He hadn't had any use for it. The very thought of returning to this incredible space where he'd spent so much of his childhood and teenage years always had him breaking out in a sweat. Just like it did now, but this time he refused to let it stop him.

Despite years of disuse, the door unlocked and opened easily. Tate had to grin. This was probably as a result of Murdoch's efforts. They'd never talked about it, but Tate knew Murdoch did many things to maintain the house and grounds. He'd disagreed with how Tate had cut himself off from others and the beauty surrounding them. Murdoch had handled upkeep on the underground cave, the beachfront and nursery. Until he'd left, he'd handled the inspections of the third floor, too. Tate had no interest in all the "history" up there. Murdoch's attempt to keep Sabatini House in livable condition was his way of voicing his opinion without having to deal with direct conflict.

The way they both liked it.

Sure enough, the furniture on the deck had been carefully covered and secured. Tate kept his gaze trained on his task without letting it stray to the water nearby. He made quick work of the preparations. Soon he'd taken the tarps off a table with two chairs and strategically placed them for viewing the approaching sunset. He prepared another side table to hold the food. When he'd told Willow they would have a nice dinner, he hadn't told her exactly where.

Tate wasn't necessarily ready to talk about commitment or permanence over the salad course, but he could no longer ignore what was happening with Willow. The emotions and sensations he experienced when they were together—both in bed and out of it—were unique. The feelings Tate had around her both scared the spit out of him *and* left him wanting more. He had to acknowledge whatever this was in some way—for his sake and hers.

He returned to the kitchen right on time. Willow already had the tray loaded to carry the serving dishes into the breakfast nook where he normally ate alone. Without a word, he relieved her of the burden. Then he loaded their place settings onto the tray as well and headed out of the kitchen.

"Where are you going?" Willow asked.

After a brief pause, he finally heard her steps as she rushed to follow him. When she caught up he stood to one side of the open French doors. Then he stepped through and led her to the seating area he had set up.

When he didn't hear her follow, he put the tray down on the side table and glanced back. She stood just outside the doorway, looking confused. He tried not to smile as he returned to her, took her hand, then led her to her seat, which faced the ocean.

"I thought you never came out here because of the bad memories," she finally said.

"Surprised?" he asked.

Her smirk was extra sassy. "You're enjoying this, aren't you?" Then her expression sobered. "But honestly, Tate, I can't believe how well you're dealing with your fear of the water."

Tate glanced at the sun as it slowly sank into the horizon, leaving the sky various shades of pink and purple. "It's time, don't you think?" He shifted his gaze to her. "I know you do. But to answer your first question, yes, I'm enjoying some of it."

"Especially shocking the pants off me," she teased.

"Oh no," he said, letting her playful tone distract him from his darker side. "There's better ways to accomplish that goal."

Her grin made him light up inside. For the first time since she'd come to Sabatini House, he served her. He set their places, then filled their plates. As they ate, Tate found he was okay as long as he didn't stare directly into the ocean and didn't allow himself to remember those heart-wrenching moments from so long ago.

Sometimes the monsters get bigger if we let them hide in the dark. One of the protagonists in his books had said that. Tate should have listened to himself a long time ago.

"Are you going to tell me what brought this on?"

Willow finally asked after about twenty minutes of small talk.

Tate allowed himself to savor his bite of beef while he formulated his answer. "You've been good for me, Willow."

"Are you sure?"

Sarcasm wasn't what he'd expected, though he should have, considering his audience.

"Yes. We both know I don't express my gratitude very well—"

"Humph."

He ignored her for the moment. "But I do appreciate all you've done here and wanted to show you I'm making an effort."

"Don't do it for me," she insisted, shaking her head. "Do it for you."

"I will. I—" For a strange moment, words failed him. "Willow, these last few weeks have been incredible—"

Her distressed squeak caught his attention.

"What is it?" he asked.

Her wide green eyes were full of worry. "Did you serve me dinner, then show me you're making positive changes, so you could tell me you don't need me anymore?"

"Is that what you want me to say?"

Now she looked confused. "No."

"Then it's a good thing that wasn't my plan."

She sat, chest heaving, face flushed. Part of him felt bad about her distress, but the other part was amused.

And flattered. At least she wanted to stay, even though he'd been a jackass on occasion.

"Then what was your plan?" she asked.

He couldn't help teasing a little more. "If you'd stop jumping to conclusions, I might be able to finish."

She gave a short nod, but he'd swear her eyes were teary before she lowered her eyelids. Time to get down to business.

"Whatever this is," he said, gesturing between the two of them, "it's different for me. Unique."

Now Willow looked up, pinning him with that green gaze. "Really?" she whispered.

Tate nodded, reaching out to finger several strands of her fiery hair. Not only did he want to touch her, but it felt weird to say this stuff without touching her. "Thank you for being here."

Somehow Tate knew the look that they shared said way more than either of them was ready to voice. "I—" He swallowed, unsure how to put these exact feelings into words. "I—"

She cut him off. "Me, too."

He knew she was getting his message, but he had to finish.

"You're incredible. And I don't really know what to do with this, but I don't want it to end." Not his most suave speech, but Tate wasn't a very suave kind of guy. Written words were much more his forte than spoken. But at least he was honest.

As his reward, she leaned forward and pressed her lips tightly against his for a few seconds.

"Is that a yes?" he asked after she pulled back.

She grinned. "You bet."

"See," he said. "I knew we had something to celebrate."

Suddenly Willow gasped. He barely had time to raise a brow before she was up and running back into the house.

He couldn't help but call out, "Did you change your mind already?"

Fourteen

Willow rushed around the kitchen, anxious to get everything ready before Tate came inside to find out why she was acting so weird. After as little time as possible, she headed back to the deck with a small tray at a much slower pace.

Tate stood to one side of the table, staring at the sky. How long had it been since he'd watched the sun set over the ocean out here? From the tight set of his shoulders, he wasn't necessarily enjoying it, and he kept back from the edge of the deck, but he was here. That was a step in the right direction. An important step in taking his life back from the shadows.

Willow hoped her surprise would be a positive step, too. "Happy Birthday, Tate."

As he turned, she looked into his eyes, then watched as his gaze dropped to the miniature cake she was carrying.

He didn't move for so long she started to panic inside. Was he angry that she'd acknowledged the birthday he hadn't celebrated in years? Then suddenly he strode toward her, took the tray and set it aside.

Just when she thought he would recant everything he'd said earlier, he cupped her face and kissed her. Unlike earlier, this kiss was slow and very, very hot.

All too soon, Tate drew back and barely whispered, "I just might love you."

Willow didn't respond, couldn't for the fear and excitement rushing through her, but she smiled before brushing her lips back across his. She wasn't ready to say it out loud, but this was enough, for now.

"Time for cake," she finally said.

To his chagrin, she made him go through the whole blowing-out-the-candle thing. No mention was made by either of them of a wish. Willow didn't want to push Tate too far. She made a silent one for him instead, in hopes he could find the happiness he deserved.

He did seem to enjoy it as they cut through the checkerboard exterior to the cake layered with chocolate ganache below. Afterward they cleared the dishes from the deck together and left it in darkness.

Willow made quick work of loading the dishwasher, anticipation sparkling in her veins. Tate only exacerbated the situation. He touched her every time he passed close until her skin grew tight, her body wet with need.

Just as she finished, he picked up the stack of clean trays and stored them back under the island, knocking her purse off the counter in the process. He bent over to pick it up.

Willow didn't realize anything was wrong until he stood and asked, "What the hell is this?"

He was holding the little white box from the pharmacy.

His voice turned hard, accusing. "You told me you took the pill."

Willow's heart pounded. Her stomach twisted so hard she thought she might be sick. "I did." She could barely get her voice above a whisper. "I just—I haven't felt right."

Tate stared at the box with what Willow could only describe as horror. For a moment, she swore he swayed. She immediately reached for him, but at the last minute he backed away and straightened. Willow wasn't sure if he was bracing himself or deliberately pulling out of her reach.

Based on his behavior since she'd met him, she assumed a bit of both. Tate had spent a lifetime alone. Isolation seemed to be his defense of choice. After the evening they'd just had, the fact that he would pull away hurt more than she wanted him to see.

But she couldn't change him.

Willow found herself frozen, unsure of what to do.

Then Tate blinked, visibly trying to get a hold of himself. "I don't understand," he murmured. "You said you took the pill."

She could accept his saying it once, but repeating himself... "Are you accusing me of lying?" she demanded.

"No," he said, drawing out the word. "I just don't understand."

She opened her mouth to tell him to get a clue, but then closed it again. "Is it that you don't understand, or that you don't want to understand?"

For the first time, he really looked at her. "What?"

Yep. Sometimes it was hard to face reality. "So I'm guessing I'm not the only one who glossed over the failure-rate information in the literature."

"I guess not."

He was too calm, speaking in a completely detached, logical tone. That was probably not a good sign, but Willow could see the first beads of sweat against his temples. He might just be human after all. Somehow it felt good to have someone else sweating over this issue, instead of just her.

"Let's do it."

Wait. What? She frowned at him as she said, "I don't understand."

Tate held up the box and shook it. "We need to take this."

"Don't you mean *I* need to take it?" she pointed out.

"Are we going to argue about semantics or pee on the dang stick?"

Oh, she could argue all night long if it meant not taking that test. "Do you really want to know?" she asked.

"The truth is there, whether we know it or not." This time his gaze was much steadier, but she had to wonder if he was hiding more extreme emotions. She knew she was.

Fear. Anger. Sadness.

"Come on." There was resolve in his voice. Clearly he wasn't shying away from the action required.

He headed down the hall, and for a moment she couldn't get her feet to follow. Part of her could have stood in the kitchen forever, rather than take the test. Finally she managed to reach the stairs just as he made it to the top. Then she trailed him into her room.

She was glad they were doing it there. For some reason, she needed the comfort of the familiar right now. And frankly his suite held too many memories for her to handle on top of this situation.

To her dismay, Tate walked straight through to the bathroom. Willow paused to take a deep breath. She needed to take control of this situation—ASAP. Otherwise Tate would think he had the only vote…and she'd find herself at his complete and total mercy.

She stopped short behind him as he stared at the box on the counter. "Out," she said.

Tate glanced up, meeting her gaze in the mirror. "But—"

"Out."

He obeyed, but stopped only a few inches outside the doorway. She had to close the door carefully but firmly. She briefly wished to use the lock, but figured it wouldn't stop him if he really wanted back inside.

At least he didn't have to break it down five minutes later when she didn't respond to his knocks. She simply couldn't make herself move, even after he let himself in. She faced the counter, hands braced, eyes squeezed shut. He closed in until his heat bathed her back. His chest brushed her as he leaned over her shoulder to look at the test on the counter.

"Okay, then."

Willow opened her eyes to see him walking away. Her stomach dropped. Glancing down, she felt her world tilt.

Can't sleep. Hot. Grumpy.

There was so much on Willow's mind—the baby, her family, the ledger, Tate. She'd only taken the test last night and already the chaos was overwhelming. In an effort to try to make some sense of any of it, she looked back through the book to make sure her dates and impressions were correct.

Unfortunately, the answers weren't waiting there on the parchment page.

What was she going to do? There was no mistaking the dates, or that this entry was somehow tied to the McLemore family. Circumstantial evidence, but the court of public opinion didn't care about those niceties. Only, if she were to reveal this, instead of just diverting blame to a family that might not care, she would be destroying the reputation of the family her child would be a part of.

Her child. She laid her hand over her stomach. It was still kind of hard to comprehend.

No longer able to lie still, Willow headed out of her room. She'd kill for some coffee. Knowing that it wouldn't taste right put her in a very bad mood.

The light in Tate's office was on. She paused but heard no sound. Had he truly been working or simply avoiding her? Should she rush inside and demand to know what he was thinking or give him his space to process, like she was doing?

It was just too hard to guess.

She wished she was like Jasmine or Ivy. They dealt with high-powered men every day. What would they have done? Willow was more suited to recalcitrant boys or know-it-all freshmen. She had logical conversations that dealt with schedules and term papers and historical facts. Not power plays or emotional issues.

Tate was a whole different animal that she'd shown very little skill in handling. So she continued on her way, figuring it best if she didn't poke the lion in its cage.

There was no point going to the kitchen. And she didn't need to start breakfast for Tate for several hours yet. Would he even come down to eat, or wait until she'd moved on to something else so he didn't have to confront her?

Antsy and anxious, she continued to the lower level. Maybe she'd start some laundry. Instead, she found herself stopping before the door to the underground cave. In the same way she'd seen Tate standing there the other night, she pressed her hand to the door, soaking in the sound of the waves. They sounded a little choppy right now with the storm arriving today. By midafternoon they'd be crashing against the shore outside, the sound drowned out by the torrential rain they were supposed to receive.

Which only served to remind her how hot she was right now. Without too much thought, she opened the door and walked through. The incredible sight drew her in. What had probably been a natural cave when Tate's ancestors first arrived had been reshaped to great effect by human ingenuity. The ceiling was low but long, with a man-made stone and copper-orange tile arch marking the front of the pool. Flicking a nearby light switch, she stepped down hand-hewn stone steps into the cool, damp room.

The few working bulbs were just enough light to let her explore safely. The light shimmered over the lapping water. With each receding wave, she could see wide long steps leading down into a roughly rectangular pool. The far end was an open frame, offering glimpses of the sky beyond, which was still dark gray before the dawn.

Fascinated, she sat on the edge, dangling her legs in the water. It felt like her entire body cooled down a degree or two. Her muscles started to relax. This had felt like the hottest summer, but especially the past few weeks. Her brain gave a mental pause before she laughed.

She wondered if being overheated had anything to do with those pregnancy hormones at work again. She guessed the next time she went to town, she needed to buy a book, huh?

The water felt so good. She'd grown up with the beach and was a strong swimmer. It felt weird to have been near a beach so long this summer and not swum at all.

Without thinking, she stood and stripped to her bra and panties. The cool water sent chills over her as she waded into it. It felt so good. She loved to swim. She missed it.

Cautiously she waded a little deeper. The cave was so large that the water was already chest high about three-quarters of the way out. There Willow started to swim from one side to the other.

Not knowing what to expect, she didn't risk getting too close to the opening to the ocean. The cave's structure slowed the water down just enough to keep the waves gentle. Willow felt her stress melt away with this simple, cool exercise. Here in the gently lapping water she didn't think about old feuds or tragedies or what to call these feelings for Tate—just about breathing, moving and the feel of the liquid chill against her skin.

Until a loud bang broke her concentration. Willow jerked upright to see Tate in the open doorway, fury on his face. She barely registered how angry he was before a cramp running down her side took her under. Her immediate panic wasn't for the water closing over her head or for the doubled-up position that kept her from standing.

It was for the vicious pain that stole her breath and her peace of mind.

Then a hard grip pulled her above the surface. She quickly found herself pressed against a fully clothed male. Tate seemed to be yelling as he dragged her back to the pool's edge.

Willow wasn't sure. She was too busy struggling to process what had just happened—oh, and suck in air.

Only when Tate plopped her butt-first on the edge did she finally start to listen. By then, the pain had disappeared. *Thank goodness.*

"Why would you do this? You know how I feel about this place. So you decide to come swim in here alone and would have drowned if I hadn't happened to walk by at that moment?" His loud voice echoed off the cave walls. Willow started to shiver.

"Why would you do this, Willow? What possessed you? I told you this place was *off-limits.*"

In that moment, Willow decided she'd had enough. Those last two words made her want to scream. Instead she clenched her teeth and ground out, "I don't know, Tate. I guess for a moment I thought I might be more than just a hired employee. You know—a woman capable of making her own decisions for a change."

"How did that work for you?" he asked, his face tight with anger. "Your foolishness could have killed our child."

Fifteen

"Don't I have any say in this?"

Tate knew he looked like a prison guard as he stood over her, legs locked, arms crossed over his chest. But he couldn't seem to soften his position. "Don't you want to know if everything is okay?"

"Is that why he's here?" Her green gaze seemed to hold an accusation that he wasn't quite catching.

"Yes, he's a doctor."

"Well, the last time you brought home a medical surprise, my well-being wasn't what you had in mind."

Light dawned. Man, they had some serious communication issues. Tate knew it. He should have talked to her instead of rushing to the phone to call

Dr. D'Ambrosio. But the shock had him more than a little off-kilter.

About everything. While Willow spent the night sleeping—in her own room—Tate had spent it pacing his office while his brain ran through all of the possibilities. Life could be such a mess sometimes.

As much as Tate argued with himself that he'd vowed never to have children, the fact was, Willow was pregnant. Obviously fate had a completely different plan from his. The question was, what did they do now?

For Tate, this was completely foreign territory. But the only emotion absent in the gamut he'd run during the long night was any desire to end this now.

What that meant, he wasn't sure. But he and Willow would figure it out together...if they could figure out how to have an actual conversation about it.

First and foremost, he had to know she was safe.

He took a deep breath and deliberately softened his tone of voice. "Please let him check you and the—" Tate was almost afraid to say it aloud. *A baby.* The emotions rolling through him left his throat tight. "Please."

Dr. D'Ambrosio smiled as if to reassure her. Tate had always liked the doctor. Even more so as he had softened with old age. His shock of white hair contrasted with deeply tanned skin that said he enjoyed being outdoors. He'd helped bring Tate and his brother into the world and tended to their sicknesses—and his brother's death—since then. They saw each other rarely, but Tate was certainly glad he could call on him right now.

"Why don't you just have a seat here," Dr. D said, indicating a chair at the breakfast nook table, "and tell me what happened."

Casting Tate another suspicious glance, Willow eased into the chair. She explained the barest of essentials about the past few weeks. The doctor glanced his way, and Tate confirmed with a nod. Yes, he was responsible. Tate found that knowledge scarier than anything he could dream up for his horror novels. Whatever happened here, he was responsible.

"And the dates?" Dr. D asked.

Had it really been four, no, five weeks?

The push and pull in his mind over Willow seemed to have gone on forever. He had made the decision to see where this could go, but as usual fate was prepared to goad him as far as absolutely possible.

The doctor took a seat in front of Willow, leaving Tate to observe.

"How are you feeling?" Dr. D'Ambrosio asked in a voice set to soothe.

"I'm not nauseated," she said with a frown. "Is that a problem?"

"No," he assured her. "I realize that's the most common symptom, but some women never have it. Anything else?"

"I'm really tired and everything tastes weird."

"Any cramps?"

"No. Not until I was in the water."

"Let's take a look at you." Using his stethoscope, the

doctor listened to her heart and lungs and stomach before he asked, "So you went swimming?"

Willow nodded.

"And went under? Can you tell me what happened?"

She glanced at Tate, as if it made her uncomfortable that he was listening, then back down at the floor. "Everything was fine. But when I jerked up out of the water, I got a cramp."

Had his unexpected arrival set that off?

"Can you show me where?" the doctor asked.

Willow placed her palm flat on her right side, then dragged it down and across her lower belly.

Tate could feel his every muscle tensing. Regardless of where, cramping wasn't good. Was it? Even more surprising was the fact that he cared. Really cared. He didn't know where the emotions were coming from, but he did know his brain thought this was a good reason to freak out.

"I see." The doctor whispered something and Willow shook her head. Tate stepped closer.

Dr. D'Ambrosio leaned back. "Let's go lie down in the living room, and I'll take a peek. Would that be okay with you?"

Willow seemed to relax under his bedside manner. She'd been tense since Tate had yelled at her. No, *tense* wasn't the right word. She was tight to the point of breaking.

It was all his fault. If he hadn't been so ugly to her,

hadn't let the high tension of his conflicting emotions get the better of him…

Dr. D'Ambrosio helped Willow up and guided her to the austere, old-fashioned couch in the living room.

"When did you find out you were pregnant?" he asked.

"I took the test last night, but I—" She lowered her eyelids while biting her lip.

"It's okay," he encouraged her. "Just tell me."

Tate understood her hesitation but was anxious to get past the interrogation. "It was a surprise because she took the morning-after pill," he said.

The doctor nodded and patted Willow's hand. "I'll be right back."

Despite his advanced age, he returned fairly quickly with a chest-high machine on four wheels. The bottom was a slick white and gray cabinet attached to a wide support post. Above that there were drawers, then a shelf with a closed laptop. The whole setup easily rolled across the hardwood floor.

"What's that?" Tate asked.

"An ultrasound machine. We'll take a look and see what's happening." He smiled down at Willow. "It may be too early. Maybe not. Okay?"

"Is it safe? Will it work?" Willow asked, her voice sounding small.

"Very," the doctor assured her. "And don't worry. Whatever is happening with you should show up. I only use the best equipment there is."

Tate moved around to stand near Willow's head as Dr. D'Ambrosio got everything ready. He opened the laptop and the screen flickered to life.

"Handy," Tate murmured, as impressed as he was surprised.

The doctor flashed him a grin, then focused on Willow. "Just relax. This won't hurt at all."

Dr. D'Ambrosio started rubbing Willow's stomach with the wand in slow circles, smoothing the clear jelly across her skin. The image on the screen just looked like shades of gray to Tate. Some spots were darker, some lighter. There was nothing that looked like a child, even a tiny one.

Finally, Dr. D'Ambrosio paused. There was a darker circle on the screen now. Along the lower curve was a small flashing light. "See that?" he asked.

"Yes," Willow whispered.

"That's your baby's heartbeat."

Willow gasped. Tate stared. His own heartbeat sped up, almost as if it were trying to match the rapid pace of the blinking light.

"It's too early to tell much," Dr. D'Ambrosio was saying. "But this is a good sign. We'll just monitor you both and see what happens."

Tate wasn't sure what other men felt when faced with the miracle of life, but he seemed to go numb. Everywhere except the beating of his heart. Even though they'd known since last night that Willow was actually pregnant, Tate felt like he'd been wrestling with nebulous what-ifs and his own assumptions.

The picture on that screen wasn't simply an object. A whole host of implications weighed Tate down. Fear. Dismay. After all, he'd told himself he'd never have children. That his family should end with him.

But as he stared at that little blinking light, the endless possibilities sparked a flare of hope inside of him. A foreign sensation, to be sure. But just like the love he felt for Willow, he recognized it without having ever felt it before.

Only he didn't know what the hell to do with either one.

The doctor swirled the wand around a little more, but Tate couldn't tell what he was looking at. Then he turned off the machine and started cleaning up the leftover gel.

Just when the panic reached a crescendo inside him, and Tate knew he'd have to leave before he did something stupid, a chilled hand slipped into his. He glanced at the sofa, but Willow wasn't looking at him. She watched the doctor intently as he finished, then helped her sit up. But her grip on Tate's hand didn't ease.

Tate found himself focusing in on her. How cold her fingers were. The slight tremble in her grip. The way she licked her lips and swallowed hard.

She's nervous.

"Will the morning-after pill hurt the baby?" she finally asked.

Then Tate realized she wasn't just nervous. She was scared. He could feel the same emotion creeping into the chaos inside him. Unsure what to do, he sat next to her. He didn't put his arm around her. He wasn't sure she'd want that. But he sat close enough to lend his warmth and adjusted his hold on her hand to encompass more of her fingers.

"I'm hoping everything will be fine," Dr. D'Ambrosio said with a calm nod, "but we'll keep a close eye on you, just in case." He reached into his bag and pulled out a bottle. "I want you to start on these prenatal vitamins. That will help with some of the fatigue."

She nodded. "Why…" She licked her lips again. In that moment, Tate could only imagine how much worse her fear was than his. After all, she was the one it was happening to. He'd been focused solely on himself, how this would affect him. His demands were so selfish when viewed in that light. "What is the cramping all about?"

"Don't you worry. From the position and the fact that you had the cramp while you were exercising, I believe its source is very simple."

"What?" Tate demanded.

Dr. D'Ambrosio grinned. "Growing pains. As your belly expands, especially for the first time, your muscles have to adjust. Sometimes they don't like that. You shouldn't have to restrict your activities unless you have more severe problems. Simply rest when it happens and see if it goes away. If it doesn't, call me. I want to make sure you stay healthy, and that the pregnancy stays viable. That could be trickier if it turns out to be twins."

"What?" she and Tate almost yelled at the same time.

The older man grinned as if he found their shock amusing. "Well, there's been a set in every Kingston generation, hasn't there?"

Tate was stunned. He couldn't move. Couldn't think.

As he packed up, Dr. D'Ambrosio added, "Congratulations to you both. I'll check in next week unless you call me."

Tate mumbled something as the doctor left, but he and Willow remained locked in place, hands clasped.

Willow woke to find herself in Tate's bed. That was confusing because she was pretty sure she'd fallen asleep on the hard, uncomfortable couch downstairs as she lay there, desperately trying to process what had just happened. Tate hadn't been joking that first night when he'd said the furniture downstairs wasn't fit for sleeping. Or relaxing, even. She'd felt almost like she was on a real table in a doctor's office while Dr. D'Ambrosio had done her ultrasound.

Ultrasound. Incredible. That tiny flashing speck had actually been a baby's heartbeat?

Her hand wandered down to press against her lower stomach. How was she going to do this? She thought back to everything she'd seen Jasmine go through over the last year with Rosie. Rosie was adopted, so Jasmine hadn't actually had to go through labor, but even without that the load had been heavy. What if Willow sucked at all of that stuff?

Without warning, she started to cry. Big fat tears rolled down her cheeks. Thankfully her weeping was silent. She was mortified that it was happening at all. She wasn't a weepy sort of person. Then the bed shifted behind her and Willow realized she had an audience.

She pressed her face into the pillow, hoping to hide the reaction since she couldn't seem to stop it.

"Willow, are you okay?"

"Are you?" she mumbled, hoping to turn the conversation away from her own inner turmoil.

"What I am doesn't matter."

That stopped her tears quick. She twisted to face him. He sat on the opposite side of the bed. The rain must have finally started, because the room was dark, even without the shutters pulled. Still she could see him very clearly in this light.

"Since when?"

"I just don't figure the man has much say in these matters."

She sat up, too, feeling at a disadvantage lying down. She tried to wipe the tears from her face as surreptitiously as possible, hoping the dimness would protect her just a touch. "I don't know about other relationships, but in this one, you do. And I expect you to express an opinion…you know, when I ask for it."

In the light of the single lamp across the room, she

saw him grin. At least they could still sass each other during this very awkward conversation.

"So this is a relationship, huh?" he asked.

That wasn't the question Willow had expected, but she refused to shy away from it. "Well, I thought that's where we were heading, but if you've changed your mind, I fully understand."

"No, Willow. I haven't changed my mind."

When she didn't respond, he went on. "I realize I lost control for a little while there. And I can't promise it won't happen again. All of this—" he waved between the two of them "—is new to me. Some of it is…scary."

"Even to renowned thriller author Adam Tate?"

"Yes, especially to him. I'm sure a psychologist would have a field day about why a man like me writes books like that, but the truth is, some of this will be scary. Please have patience with me."

"Me, too."

He raised a single brow.

"I've never done the relationship thing… At least, romantically."

"I find that hard to believe."

Willow shook her head. "I'm very close with my family, so I do know some things about relationships. But I've never dated much…never long-term. And I have helped a lot with my sister's adopted daughter, Rosie, so I'm not totally clueless about babies."

Even if the thought of having a baby of her own was terrifying. Exhilarating, too, but the fear muted everything else for the moment. The thought of doing it all alone didn't put her at ease, either. She didn't think Tate was into being a hands-on dad.

"I'm glad one of us will know what we're doing. You'll have to teach me."

Surprised, Willow stared.

Tate met her gaze for a moment, then turned away with an uncomfortable look on his face. "I'm warning you, I will probably completely suck as a father. But if nothing else, I'll be there for monetary support."

Uh, no. He'd already hinted at an interest in raising the child. She wasn't going to let him back down now. "That's not acceptable," she informed him.

His gaze snapped back to hers. "What?"

"You are a smart, sensitive man. Creative. Imaginative. I expect you to put all of those traits to work for our baby. The last thing we need is your ancestors having the last word and the child turning out like them, right? I'd much prefer he or she turn out like you."

Time seemed to freeze for a moment, then Tate gave a huff of laughter. "As I said, you're incredible."

"I'm just smart," Willow said with a shrug.

In the blink of an eye, Tate was across the bed and using his weight to bear her back down to the mattress. "And sexy," he growled as he buried his face into her neck.

Something had been bugging her since she woke up. Willow finally remembered what it was. "Tate, I really need to call my sisters."

"There's plenty of time for that," he murmured against her.

He was completely focused on one thing, so she added, "Before the landline fails."

"If you're really nice, I'll let you use my satellite phone."

Even as she giggled, she reached to his side and pinched him.

"Ouch!" he said, jerking back a little. "That's not nice!"

She gave him a big, cheesy smile. "There's more where that came from."

"Not if I sweeten you up first."

"Not happening," she teased, but had a feeling Tate would make her eat those words.

Easing her over, he started by removing her shirt and bra, then initiated long, steady strokes up and down her back. Just the right amount of pressure. Just the right speed. Willow felt like she was melting into the mattress.

Very few things had ever felt this good.

Then he started in on her arms, squeezing the muscles and massaging her hands. Her moans mingled with the sound of rain as it started to pelt the windows. He moved on to her legs after removing the rest of her clothes. Willow tried to lighten the mood before she completely lost her mind.

"Just for future reference," she gasped, struggling to form words.

"Yes?" he asked, but he didn't stop massaging her calves.

What was she saying? *Oh, right.* "Your talent in the bedroom makes up for a multitude of sins."

Finally he covered her back, surprising her with his bare chest against her. He whispered in her ear, "I'll definitely keep that in mind."

He turned her over, so they were face-to-face, and continued his gentle, thorough attentions. Willow soaked up his touch. His intensity broke through any physical barriers to stroke her very soul. Any hesitation she'd felt to this point was immediately burned away.

By the time he joined them together, Willow was lost. There was nothing left standing between them. Naked in every way possible, Willow opened up to him. She lifted to meet his every stroke. Tate's focus and intensity pushed her higher until she leaped over the edge without a second thought. His heavy thrusts and harsh cries sent her over again.

She resurfaced to the feel of his pounding heart beneath her palm and the knowledge that she'd never be the woman she'd been before. It was almost too much. Too raw.

Maybe for him, too. He rolled away, sprawling on the other side of the bed. To her surprise, he didn't break their connection, though. His hand came to rest on her forearm and he didn't pull it away. They lay for long moments, the only sound in the room their own harsh breathing.

Finally, desperate to break the silence, Willow teased, "I don't remember any sex scenes in the Adam Tate books. Where'd you learn to do that?"

Tate grunted, not quite as recovered as she was. It took some time before he said, "I'm an author. I have a more vivid imagination than most."

As she giggled, he rolled back to hug her close. For at least a few moments, everything was right in Willow's world.

Sixteen

A bang, then muffled cursing woke Willow from her afternoon nap. Dr. D'Ambrosio had told her sleeping for a short while in the afternoons might help with the exhaustion. Luckily her employer had no complaints. After lunch, cleaning and a long three-way call with her sisters, Willow had lain down in her bedroom.

She still had to clean up some minor debris on the front deck and remove the lower-level shutters from the windows, but otherwise, they'd had very little damage from the storm. Not that they would have noticed if the house had come down around them. She and Tate had spent most waking moments during the stormy weekend in bed together. "Bonding time," he'd laughingly called it.

And she very much feared he'd created a bond she would never be able to break. This new, lighter side of Tate was a wonderful thing, beautiful and freeing. She knew better than to think the darker side had disappeared. She only hoped this happiness remained a part of him forever.

The room had gone silent again, but Willow could sense Tate's presence. She opened her eyes to see him staring at the floor. "What is it?" she asked.

He bent down and didn't come back up. The silence was too pervasive. After a few seconds, Willow sat up and stared at his back. "Tate? What's wrong?"

He stood up, then dropped something flat on the bed. The ledger. As her stomach sank, Willow had a feeling playtime was now over.

Without a word, Tate opened the book and leafed through the first few pages. His expression remained impassive when she'd have given anything to know what he was thinking. Then again, when he spoke she wished he hadn't.

"Is this another example of *I'm more than an employee so I can go wherever I want*?"

Ouch. But Willow couldn't fault him for saying it.

As much as she didn't think she was ready for this, there was no point in beating around the bush. "No, Tate. I found the keys you used to let the workmen upstairs."

"And just made yourself at home?"

"No, that wasn't—"

"What is this? Why would you want it?"

He flipped through the pages until he came to the one marked with a sticky note. Obviously those weren't around at the time the ledger had been written, so… He glanced up at her before reading the page.

"I still don't understand," he said. "Why would something like this be of interest to you?" He read some more. "It's just a contract for a random business transaction."

Willow stood up, seriously wishing she had on decent clothes for this confrontation rather than just her comfy shirt and shorts. "Actually, that date is very important. It's the day the McLemore ship was burned, with their male heir inside."

That gave Tate pause. He flipped back a few pages and read them. Then he flipped forward a few more. His jaw went tight. "So, this is a ledger of my ancestor's misdeeds? Why would anyone care about that in this day and age?"

Good question. "Well, that's a little complicated."

He braced himself, arms crossed over his chest. "Try me."

"My sister is pregnant with Paxton McLemore's child. The matriarch of the family was a little girl when her uncle was killed aboard that ship."

Tate frowned at that news.

"The people accused of perpetrating the crime were run out of town by the McLemores, who harassed them endlessly with sabotage of their business and personal threats. That family line is now continued in the Hardens. My Hardens."

She'd expected more questions, but Tate simply stared down at the open book before him.

Willow hurried to fill the silence. "I just didn't want my family, my sister, to be falsely accused. To be held accountable for something our family didn't do."

"But it's okay to implicate mine?"

Willow threw her hands up. "There's no good way to answer that, Tate. I've been struggling with the right choice since I found the ledger. I simply can't figure out what it is."

How could she explain this better? "At first, I only wanted to see if there was any information from that time out of curiosity. So we as a family could confirm what I found in my great-grandmother's journals. Some things Murdoch told me led me to believe..."

Willow could swear Tate paled five shades lighter. His expression went cold, just as his lips pressed tightly together. "You came here just to find this book?"

"Not that book specifically..."

"You came here to spy on me?" he clarified.

Knowing what he must be thinking made her ache inside. "Technically I had a job, but—"

Tate slammed the book shut, causing her to jump. In comparison, his voice was deadly quiet. "But you came here for this."

"I told you, I was simply curious, at first," she defended herself. "Then I found out my sister was pregnant, and things got complicated."

"I'll bet."

"Tate—"

She bristled at the way he held up his hand for silence. Even though she knew he had a right to be angry, his refusal to listen was totally ticking her off.

"My family lived off deceit," he said. "I told you from the beginning how they were, what they did. They didn't have very nice reputations, and the word *murderer* might have actually applied a time or two in the earlier generations.

"I told you I didn't want to live like that. Refused to live like they had. And yet deceit is exactly what you brought here."

She refused to let him brand her that way. "Tate, I did not know what would happen here. How life would change from the first moment I walked through the doors of Sabatini House. I love my family. I was trying to help them. But…I love you."

He picked up the oversize book with a white-knuckled grip. "Then what is this doing here? If you loved me, why would you do exactly what I asked you not to?"

"Because I had decisions to make, Tate. I didn't know what to do. I wanted to hold on to the book until I could figure out what was best."

"Well, I'll make the decision for you, then," he said, dropping the book back onto the bed with a thump. The look he sent her had the hardest edge she'd seen from him. "Get out."

* * *

Tate sank into his office chair, dropping the stack of mail onto his desk next to the ledger. The stack was huge. He was used to having it brought to him every day and he'd forgotten that he now needed to go check the mailbox. It had been only a week, but it was long enough for him to see that both Murdoch and Willow had been culling the mail before bringing it to him.

Why in the world would anyone need so many advertisements?

He stared, feeling every bit of his irritation focused on the mail, even though logic told him that wasn't what was influencing his mood. Finally, he turned his gaze to the old, leather-bound ledger next to it. He'd found it on Willow's neatly made bed after she left.

He'd managed to stay away from the room for two days, but eventually couldn't keep himself from it any longer. He simply had to see if she'd left anything behind. And she had.

He just hadn't been able to accept her explanation. She knew how he'd felt about his family's actions. He felt so strongly that he'd cut himself off from relationships to eliminate the possibility of that behavior continuing through an heir.

To know that she came there for the express purpose of finding dirt on his family was just something he couldn't reconcile. At least, he didn't know how.

Since she'd been gone he'd been trapped in a kind of inertia, unable to motivate himself to work, or do much more than stare out that window...thinking. He knew he needed to hire a new housekeeper, and had even looked up a temp agency's phone number online, but he hadn't been able to make himself dial the phone.

The house was quiet, too quiet. He could feel the emptiness, but he had no idea what to do about it. Bringing in a new housekeeper wasn't going to change that.

And then there was the baby—the very last thing he wanted to think about. Did he want to have anything to do with the child if he couldn't have his mother? Did he need to just get over himself? Could he handle being nothing more than the person who sent a check once a month?

Hoping to shake off the endless rounds of questions he seemed to be stuck in with no answers, Tate sorted through the mail. His contract should be in soon. As he glanced through the various envelopes, one with familiar handwriting caught his eye.

Sure enough, in the upper right-hand corner was Murdoch's name. For just a moment, that feeling of emptiness lifted. Tate slit the envelope open and pulled out a card from inside.

A birth announcement.

Tate stared at the photo of the softly rounded baby face for a long time. It was the main picture on the front cover of the card; there were two other pictures to the side. One was of a man and woman holding the baby. The other showed the baby and the woman with Murdoch standing beside her, his arm around her shoulders.

It was hard for Tate to picture his friend in such a happy familial setting. Neither of them had a lot of experience with it. But Murdoch seemed to be learning the ropes fairly quickly.

Finally, Tate opened the card and scanned the details of the birth announcement inside, but he kept returning back to that first large picture. A baby. So vulnerable, yet so indistinct. An unclear bundle of potential, containing the makings of the adult he would be some day.

How amazing.

To think back to that single little blip of light on Willow's ultrasound and know that it would one day be a baby like this one, a teenager like his brother had been, an adult like he was now, or a grandfather like Murdoch. Just the thought unlocked the inertia that had kept Tate cocooned from his pain.

To his dismay, a mixture of emotions started to seep through the cracks. Bad ones he hadn't wanted to recognize. Good ones he hadn't wanted to remember.

As he went to return the card to its envelope, Tate noticed a little piece of paper. He pulled it out and read Murdoch's scrawled note.

I was a fool to leave her for so long. Don't make my same mistakes. The past is what it is. But the future is all up to us.

Tate dropped the note on the desk. Restless energy forced him to his feet, got him moving. He crossed over to the arched windows and found himself staring down at the beach. He'd opened the shutters right after the

storm and never closed them. As much as he wanted to
say that overcoming his fear and aversion to the water
had nothing to do with Willow, he knew he was lying
to himself. Any thoughts of his brother still hurt, but
simply looking at the water didn't anymore. And that
was a miracle.

But as much as he wanted to believe Murdoch, to believe that the potential of the future was worth letting
go of the past, Tate wasn't sure that he could.

Frustrated, he stalked back to the ledger. Why did
she leave it? Didn't she need it anymore? It would just
be her word against his if she took the information public. Did he even care about that?

He didn't know. Because he hadn't bothered to find
out any answers past the accusations. Which was his
typical MO with Willow. He'd pushed, but hadn't asked
much. Heck, he hadn't even known her parents were
dead for how long?

Idly he flipped through the book until he reached
the page she had marked. He immediately noticed the
sticky note was no longer blank. The brief message, in
Willow's elegant handwriting, contained an address
with the words: *If you ever need me, please let me know.*

For the first time, Tate looked at the long years ahead
of him and wondered about the things that he could
change, that he and his brother had always wanted to
be different but couldn't do anything about. Deep down
he knew it was time for action rather than hiding behind excuses.

It took Tate only a few minutes to change his clothes, and then he rushed down the stairs and grabbed his keys. He didn't want to give himself too much time to think, because that could lead to no action at all.

He fired up the Jeep, checked all the levels and backed out of the garage.

It wasn't until he reached the fork in the road that he acknowledged he had a choice to make. Left, and he would drive across the island to the hangar and stay safe and secure in his own little world. He could write his stories with their touch of danger while staying safely tucked away in Sabatini House for the rest of his life.

The path he always took.

Or right, and he could head down the hill to the bridge that led to the mainland. He hadn't crossed it since he was eighteen years old. He didn't even fly out that way. But he could today. He could find Willow and tell her he'd been a fool.

There was a big risk involved, especially for a man like him. One who didn't do risk. One who lived out all his adventures in the written word alone. But if he didn't take it, he would never again touch her silky skin or smell that soothing vanilla scent. Never bury himself in the heat of her body and forget the pain of the past.

Tate also thought about that soft baby face, and the picture of the mom and dad holding their child close. That's what he wanted for his child, and he hoped to God he was the type of man to give it to him. So he turned the Jeep right, took a deep breath and put it in Drive.

Seventeen

Willow finished up the beans and potato salad, while Royce took the last of the barbecue chicken off the grill. Cooking in the kitchen of the house where'd she'd spent most of her life made her foray to the island seem almost like a dream…though she was experiencing enough pregnancy symptoms to make it very real.

Auntie and Jasmine entertained the baby over at the table, while Ivy lay down after her long day searching for work. With two pregnant ladies in the house, Jasmine and Royce had been nice enough to come over a couple of times this week with dinner, instead of just the usual Sundays.

Plus, it gave everyone a chance to play with little Rosie.

At least these family dinners helped Willow not to feel so alone. A week had passed since she'd left Sabatini House. So many times throughout each day her mind was haunted by that moment of holding Tate's hand as they watched their baby's heartbeat. Even though they'd both had their own doubts and fears, in that one moment they had been united.

Instead she'd now be going it alone.

Royce came through the door from the back porch and set the platter of meat on the counter next to the stove. Then he walked over to the table and swept Rosie up into the air. Her high-pitched squeal echoed through the room. Just the reaction her daddy was going for.

Royce's transformation from cold businessman to loving father was nothing short of miraculous. Sometimes Willow could hardly believe it. If she hadn't really seen it in person, no one could have convinced her.

She and Ivy had discussed a couple of times how they were both a little envious of Jasmine, but they would figure out their relationship woes somehow. One thing was certain: the heirloom ring hadn't worked for either of them the way it had for Jasmine.

But Jasmine and Royce's path to happiness hadn't been the typical straightforward one, so Willow and Ivy weren't about to begrudge them the wonderful life they were now enjoying. It had taken a lot of effort to achieve.

To Willow, both the effort and the result were beautiful things.

As if she knew exactly what Willow was thinking, Jasmine met her gaze. "How are you doing?" she asked.

Good question. Some days she wasn't really sure. "I'm managing," she said, keeping it short and sweet.

What else could she say? She almost wished summer were over, so she'd have her teaching job to distract her. Instead she simply found whatever she could to keep herself busy, and she spent the evenings reading so she didn't waste hours wondering how Tate was and if he hated her still.

"Have you heard from Tate?"

"No. And I don't imagine I will."

"Give him time," Royce said. "He'll come around."

Willow wished she could believe that.

"Like you did?" Jasmine asked, grinning over at him.

"Yes, ma'am. We men might be slow, but we eventually recognize when we're missing a good thing." For good measure, Royce brushed a kiss over Rosie's dark, curly hair, and then did the same for her mama.

Willow wasn't so sure. Tate had barely been off that island in over twenty years. She had serious doubts about him coming for her now.

Jasmine headed down the hall to let Ivy know dinner was ready. They all gathered around the table as usual, bringing on that secure, comfortable feeling of having Willow's loved ones around her. The split was probably for the best, she thought as she looked around. Tate wouldn't ever want to be a true part of her family.

He was too isolated. And her sisters and Auntie were something she simply couldn't live without.

Suddenly, the doorbell rang.

"Who in heaven is that?" Auntie asked, craning to see out the curtain-draped windows.

"I'll get it," Ivy said. She stepped out of the room for a minute and they all heard the front door open.

"Must not have been a salesman," Royce said with a secretive smile. "Last Saturday she about bit the head off one when he interrupted her nap with his persistent knocking."

"Better keep that in mind when you go to have a brother or sister for little Rosie there," Auntie said with a cackle.

Royce's brows shot up straight to his hairline. "Not anytime soon, I hope."

Jasmine just laughed.

Finally, Ivy came back into the room, her face flushed.

"You have a visitor, Willow."

"Me?" *Who would be here to see me?*

Ivy just nodded. "I think you'd better come."

Willow found herself reluctantly heading to the front parlor. Who in the world did she know who would bother them at dinnertime?

She gasped as she rounded the corner and saw Tate standing on the front porch. At first, seeing him was so out of context that her brain refused to register who it was. Then Ivy passed her with a glass of water. She stepped through the door, where she handed it over to Tate. He drew in a deep breath as if trying to steady himself before he tilted his dark head back and drank, giving Willow time to take in his olive skin and tall, familiar build.

As he finished, she could see he was deeply shaken but forcing himself to hold it together. She'd seen that expression a time or two before today. She'd be perfectly happy to never see him struggle this hard again.

The smile he gave her sister was really more of a stretching of his lips, but he murmured his thanks. Ivy stepped through the door and paused beside Willow. "He looked rough, so I thought he could use some water."

"Thanks, Ivy," Willow said, both for her thoughtfulness and for giving Willow a moment to gather her courage.

Then Ivy headed back to the kitchen, leaving Willow with no choice but to walk through the front door and stand face-to-face with a man she never thought would show up at her house.

"What are you doing here?" she asked, her voice trembling and weaker than she would have liked.

He stood with the glass in his hands, absently rubbing it like he was summoning a genie to make a wish. "I came to see you," he answered. His gaze, his voice, everything about him was direct. This was a man who knew what he was doing, even if he wasn't entirely comfortable doing it.

"Why?" Willow crossed her arms over her chest. The ache caused by the slight pressure on her breasts only reminded her how much unfinished business they had. Was the baby his reason for being here? His *only* reason?

Tate stepped closer, his grip tightening. "I need you, Willow."

"You what?" Of all the things she'd expected him to say, that wasn't one of them.

"You said if I ever needed you, this was where you'd be. Well, I do."

When she'd left that note, she'd been leaving open a door, but she'd never expected him to walk through it because of her. The baby, yes. Willow shook her head. "I guess this just isn't matching up with the Tate that I know."

"It's not the Tate I know, either," he said with a little grin. Then it faded as he swallowed hard. "But I can't do it, Willow. I can't live with the emptiness, the isolation anymore. Just me and the people who run around in my brain. I need you to make it all come alive, to make it worth doing. You and—" he gestured toward her stomach "—that little one that's beaten all the odds just to make it here."

It all sounded so good, but Willow had been burned before by him. "You said you can't live with the deceit."

"And when are you going to figure out the lie I told to protect myself? You're too smart for that." He set the glass down on the windowsill. His fists clenched and released as if he wanted to reach for her, but he kept his distance. "Claiming you deliberately deceived me was an excuse in the heat of the moment. Your actions disappointed me, so I lashed out, but I know you, Willow. You're nothing like my parents or my grandparents. If it wasn't for you pushing my boundaries, nothing would've ever changed."

"I know," she said.

"And now, so do I." His look held such longing, Willow felt tears prick her eyes. "I'm not going to pretend I don't have a lot of faults. We both know I do. But you bring out the best in me. I wouldn't be able to live with myself if I didn't take the chance that you could love me, at least a little."

Goodness, she'd have trouble holding back the waterworks if he kept talking like this. "Oh, I think I can manage a little more than that."

One step at a time he came to her, until he could finally bury his hands in her hair and study her face up close. "You really mean that?" he asked.

"Hasn't anything I've done convinced you?"

His kiss was sure, with a touch of reverence like Willow had never felt before.

"I promise to stop living in the past," he murmured. "I want a future, Willow. But the only future worth having is with you."

"We'll make it together, Tate. I promise."

"Your life will never be the same, buddy," Royce yelled out the kitchen window.

Tate and Willow turned to see a handful of faces on the other side of the curtains. She'd completely forgotten about her family, and she wanted to laugh. Eavesdropping was something she should have expected of them. But she glanced up to see Tate's eyes go wide. At first she thought he had a problem. Then she realized he was actually nervous. That was a new look for the forceful man she was used to seeing.

"Might as well get used to it," Willow warned. "We come as a package deal. You're stuck with them now."

He seemed to swallow down his nerves and nodded resolutely. "A new future. A new family. With you right at the center. Sounds like everything I didn't know I wanted. Now I can't imagine living without any of it."

"You won't. Not if you're smart." And she knew he was, or else he'd have never gotten this far. "But don't worry, they'll love you just as much as I do. As much as Murdoch does. All you have to do is let them."

Tate nodded. "I will."

It wouldn't be easy for him, not after all he'd been through, but she knew they'd get there.

Probably time to address the elephant on their front porch before Willow got too emotional. "How did you get here? Did someone bring you?" She glanced around for a taxi.

Tate took a few steps back and gestured to the Jeep parked along the curb. One she should have recognized, but didn't at first, just as she'd never expected Tate on her doorstep… "I drove."

"You what?" she whispered, shock still rocketing through her.

"I needed to see you," he said with a shrug. The explanation was so simple, but oh so profound. "Right then. I couldn't wait."

He grinned, that sexy, mysterious smile that sent shivers down her spine. On that night months ago when he'd caught her on the stairs of Sabatini House, she'd never imagined she'd be on the receiving end of something so special.

"Besides, you don't have a landing strip in your backyard, I'm guessing."

Willow laughed. "No. No, we don't."

"We might have to remedy that."

* * * * *

Notorious playboy Nolan Madaris is determined to escape his great-grandmother's famous matchmaking schemes, but Ivy Chapman, the woman his great-grandmother has picked out for him, is nothing like he expects—and she's got her own proposal for how to get their meddling families off their backs and out of their love lives!

Read on for a sneak peek of
BEST LAID PLANS,
the latest in New York Times *bestselling author*
Brenda Jackson's
MADARIS FAMILY SAGA!

Prologue

Christmas Day

Nolan Madaris III took a sip of his beer while standing on the balcony of his condo. Leaning against the rail, he had a breathtaking view of the exclusive fifteen-story Madaris Building that was surrounded by a cluster of upscale shops, restaurants and a beautiful jogging park with a huge man-made pond. The condos where he lived were right across from the water.

The entire complex, including the condos, had been architecturally designed, engineered and constructed by the Madaris Construction Company that was owned by his cousins Blade and Slade. For the holidays, the Madaris Building and the surrounding shops, restaurants and jogging park were beautifully decorated with colorful, bright lights. It was hard to believe a new year was just a week away.

When Nolan had arrived home from his cousin Lee's wedding, he hadn't bothered to remove his tuxedo. Instead he'd headed straight for the refrigerator, grabbed a beer and proceeded to the balcony for a bit of mental relaxation. But all his mind could do was recall the moment his ninetysomething-year-old great-grandmother, Felicia Laverne Madaris, had finally cornered him at the reception that evening. She was a notorious matchmaker, and he'd been avoiding her all night. Her success rate was too astounding to suit him—and she had calmly warned him that he was next.

He was just as determined not to be.

Nolan, his brother, Corbin, and his cousins Reese and Lee had all been born within a fifteen-month period. They were as close as brothers and had been thick as thieves while growing up. Mama Laverne swore her goal was to marry them all off before she took her last breath. They all told her that wouldn't happen, but then the next thing they knew, Reese had married Kenna and today Lee married Carly.

What bothered Nolan more than anything about his great-grandmother setting her schemes on him was that she of all people knew what he'd gone through with Andrea Dunmire. Specifically, the hurt, pain and humiliation she had caused him. Yes, it had been years ago and he had gotten over it, but there were some things you didn't forget. A woman ripping your heart out of your chest was one of them.

His cell phone rang. Recognizing the ringtone, he pulled it out of his pocket and answered, "Yes, Corbin?"

"Hey, man, I just wanted to check on you. We saw you tear out of here like the devil himself was after you. It's Christmas and we thought you would stay the night at Whispering Pines and continue to party like the rest of us."

Whispering Pines was their uncle Jake's ranch. Nolan took another sip of his beer before saying, "I couldn't stay knowing Mama Laverne is already plotting my downfall. You wouldn't believe what she told me."

"We weren't standing far away and heard."

Nolan shook his head in frustration. "So now all of you know that Mama Laverne's friend's granddaughter is the woman she's picked out for me."

"Yes, and we got a name. Reese and I overheard Mama Laverne tell Aunt Marilyn that your future wife's name is Ivy Chapman."

"Like hell the woman is my future wife." And Nolan couldn't care less about her name. He'd never met her and didn't intend to. "All this time I thought Mama Laverne was plotting to marry the woman's granddaughter off to Lee. She set me up real good."

Corbin didn't say anything and Nolan was glad because for the moment he needed the silence. It didn't matter to him one iota that so far every one of his cousins whose wives had been selected by his great-grandmother were madly in love with their spouses and saw her actions as a blessing and not a curse. What mattered was that she should not have interfered in the process. And what bothered him more than anything was knowing that he was next on her list. He didn't want her to find him a wife. When and if he was ready for marriage, he was certainly capable of finding one on his own.

"You've come up with a plan?" Corbin interrupted Nolan's thoughts to ask.

Nolan thought of the diabolical plan his cousin Lee had put in place to counteract their great-grandmother's shenanigans and guaranteed to outsmart Mama Laverne for sure. However, in the end, Lee's plan had backfired.

"No, why waste my time planning anything? I simply refuse to play the games Mama Laverne is intent on playing. What I'm going to do is ignore her foolishness and enjoy my life as the newest eligible Madaris bachelor."

He could say that since, at thirty-four, he was ten months older than Corbin, who would be next on their great-grandmother's hit list. "By the time I make my rounds, there won't be a single woman living in Houston who won't know I'm not marriage material," Nolan added.

Corbin chuckled. "That sounds like a plan to me."

"Not a plan, just stating my intentions. I refuse to let Mama Laverne shove a wife that I don't want down my throat just because she thinks she can and that she should."

After ending the call with his brother, Nolan swallowed the last of his beer. Like he'd told Corbin, he didn't have a plan and wouldn't waste time coming up with one. What he intended to do was to have fun; as much fun as any single man could possibly have.

A huge smile touched his lips as he left the balcony. Walking into his condo, he headed for his bedroom. Quickly removing the tux, he changed into a pair of slacks and a pullover sweater. The night was still young and there was no reason for him not to go out and celebrate the holiday.

As he moved toward his front door, he started humming "Jingle Bells." *Let the fun begin.*

One

Fifteen months later...

Nolan clicked off his mobile phone, satisfied with the call he'd just ended with Lee about his cousin's newest hotel, the Grand MD Paris. Construction of the huge mega-structure had begun three weeks ago. Already it was being touted by the media as the hotel of the future, and Nolan would have to agree.

Due to the hotel's intricate design and elaborate formation, the estimated completion time was two years. You couldn't rush grandeur, and by the time the doors opened, the Grand MD Paris would set itself apart as one of the most luxurious hotels in the world.

This would be the third hotel Lee and his business

partner, DeAngelo Di Meglio, had built. First there had been the Grand MD Dubai, and after such astounding success with that hotel, the pair had opened the Grand MD Vegas. Since both hotels had been doing extremely well financially, a decision was made to build a third hotel in Paris. The Grand MD Paris would use state-of-the-art technology while maintaining the rich architectural designs Paris was known for.

Slade, the architect in the Madaris family, had designed all three Grand MD hotels. Nolan would have to say that Slade's design of the Paris hotel was nothing short of a masterpiece. Slade had made sure that no Grand MD hotel looked the same and that each had its own unique architecture and appeal. Slade's twin, Blade, was the structural engineer and had spent the last six months in Paris making sure the groundwork was laid before work on the hotel began. There had been surveys that needed to be completed, soil samples to analyze, as well as a tight construction schedule if they were to meet the deadline for a grand opening two years from now. And knowing Lee and DeAngelo like he did, Nolan expected the Grand MD Paris to open its doors on time and to a fanfare of the likes of a presidential inauguration.

After getting a master's graduate degree at MIT, Nolan had begun working for Chenault Electronics at their Chicago office. Chenault Electronics was considered one of the top ten electronics companies in the world. The owner, Nicholas Chenault, was a family friend, had taken Nolan under his wing and had not only been his boss but his mentor, as well.

After working for Chenault for eight years, Nolan had returned to Houston three years ago to start his own company, Madaris Innovations.

Nolan's company would provide all the electronic and technology work for the Grand MD Paris; some would be the first of its kind anywhere. All high-tech and trend changing. It would be Nolan's first project of this caliber and he appreciated Lee and DeAngelo for giving him the opportunity. Lee and his wife, Carly, spent most of their time in Paris now. Since DeAngelo and his wife, Peyton, were expecting their first child four months from now, DeAngelo had decreased his travel schedule somewhat.

Nolan also appreciated Nicholas for agreeing to partner with him on the project. Chenault Electronics would be bringing years of experience and know-how to the table and Nolan welcomed Nicholas's skill and knowledge.

Nolan had enjoyed the two weeks he'd spent in Paris. He would have to go back a number of times this year for more meetings and he looked forward to doing so, since Paris was one of his favorite places to visit. There was a real possibility that he might have to live there while his electronic equipment was scheduled to be installed.

Nolan leaned back in his chair. In a way, he regretted returning to Houston. Before leaving, he had done everything in his power to become the life of every party, and his reputation as Houston's number one playboy had been cemented. In some circles, he'd been pegged as Houston's One-Night Stander. Now that he was back, that role had to be rekindled, but if he was honest with himself, he wasn't looking forward to the nights of mindless, emotionless sex with women whose names he barely remembered. He only hoped that Ivy Chapman, her grandmother and his great-grandmother were getting the message—he had no intentions of settling down anytime soon. At least not in the next twenty-five years or so.

He rubbed a hand down his face, thinking that while he wouldn't admit to it, he was discovering that living the life of a playboy wasn't all that it was cracked up to be. Most of his dates were one-night stands. There were times he would spend a week with the same woman, and occasionally someone would make it a month, but he didn't want to give these women the wrong idea about the possibility of a future together. He was probably going to have to change his phone number due to the number of messages from women wanting a callback. Women expecting a callback. Women he barely remembered from one sexual encounter to the next. Jeez.

Nolan wondered how his cousins Clayton and Blade, the ones who'd been known as die-hard womanizers in the family before they'd settled down to marry, had managed it all. Clayton had had such an active sex life that he'd owned a case of condoms that he'd kept in his closet. Nolan knew that tidbit was more fact than fiction, since he'd seen the case after Clayton had passed it on to Blade when Clayton had gotten married.

Blade hadn't passed the box on to anyone when he'd married. Not only had he used up the case he'd gotten from Clayton, but he'd gone through a case of his own. Somehow Clayton and Blade had not only managed to handle the playboy life, but each claimed they'd enjoyed doing so immensely at the time.

Nolan, on the other hand, was finding the life of a Casanova pretty damn taxing and way too demanding. And it wasn't even deterring Ivy Chapman.

Nolan picked up the envelope on top of the stack on his desk. He knew what it was and who it had come from. He recalled getting the first one six months ago and he had received several more since then. He wondered why Ivy Chapman was still sending him these little personal notes when he refused to acknowledge them. All the notes said the same thing… *Nolan, I would love to meet you. Call me so it can be arranged. Here is my number…*

Nolan didn't give a royal flip what her phone number was, since he had no intentions of calling her, regardless of the fact that his matchmaking great-grandmother fully expected him to do so. He would continue to ignore Miss Chapman and any correspondence she sent him. He refused to give in to his great-grandmother's matchmaking shenanigans.

He tossed the envelope aside and picked up his cell

phone to call his family and let them know he was back. He had slept off jet lag most of yesterday and hadn't talked to anyone other than his cousin Reese and his brother, Corbin. Reese and his wife, Kenna, were expecting their first baby in June and everyone was excited. For years, Reese and Kenna, who'd met in college, had claimed they were nothing but best friends. However, the family had known better and figured one day the couple would reach the same conclusion. Mama Laverne bragged that they were just another one of her success stories.

Nolan ended the call with his parents, stood and walked over to the window to look out. Like most of his relatives, he leased space in the Madaris Building. His electronics company was across the hall from Madaris Explorations, owned by his older cousin Dex.

He loved Houston in March, but it always brought out dicey weather. You had some warm days, but there were days when winter refused to fade into the background while spring tried emerging. He was ready for warmer days and couldn't wait to spend time at the cottage he'd purchased on Tiki Island, a village in Galveston, last year. He'd hired Ron Siskin, a property manager, to handle the leasing of the cottage whenever he wasn't using it. So far it had turned out to be not only a great investment but also a getaway place whenever he needed a break from the demands of his job, life itself and, yes, of course, the women who were becoming more demanding by the hour.

The buzzer sounded and he walked back over to his desk. "Yes, Marlene?" Marlene was an older woman in her sixties who'd worked for him since he started the company three years ago. A retired administrative assistant for an insurance agent, Marlene had decided to come out of retirement when she'd gotten bored. She was good at what she did and helped to keep the office running when he was in or out of it.

"There's a woman here to see you, Mr. Madaris. She doesn't have an appointment and says it's important."

Nolan frowned, glancing at his watch. It's wasn't even ten in the morning. Who would show up at his office without an appointment and at this hour? There were a number of family members who worked in the Madaris Building. Obviously, it wasn't one of them; otherwise Marlene would have said so. "Who is she?"

"A Miss Ivy Chapman."

He guessed she was tired of sending notes that went unanswered. Hadn't she heard around town what a scoundrel he was? The last man any woman should be interested in? So what was she doing here?

There was only one way to find out. If she needed to know why he hadn't responded, that he could certainly tell her. She could stop sending him those notes or else he would take her actions as a form of harassment. He had no problem telling her in no uncertain terms that he was not interested in pursuing an affair with her, regardless of the fact that his great-grandmother and her grandmother wanted it to be so.

"Send her in, Marlene."

"Yes, Mr. Madaris."

Nolan had eased into his jacket and straightened his tie before his office door swung open. The first thing he saw was a huge bouquet of flowers that was bigger than the person carrying them. Why was the woman bringing him flowers? Did she honestly think a huge bouquet of flowers would work when her cute little notes hadn't?

He couldn't see the woman's face behind the huge vase of flowers, and without saying a word, not even so much as a good morning, she plopped the monstrosity onto his desk with a loud thump. It was a wonder the vase hadn't cracked. Hell, maybe it had. He could just imagine water spilling all over his desk.

Nolan looked from the flowers that were taking up entirely too much space on his desk to the woman who'd unceremoniously placed them there. He was not prepared for the beauty of the soft brown eyes behind a pair of thick-rimmed glasses or the perfect roundness of her face and the creamy cocoa coloring of her complexion. And he couldn't miss the fullness of her lips that were pursed tight in anger.

"I'm only going to warn you but this once, Nolan Madaris. Do not send me any more flowers. Doing so won't change a thing. I've decided to come tell you personally, the same thing I've repeatedly told your great-grandmother and my grandmother. There is no way I'd ever become involved with you. No way. Ever."

Her words shocked him to the point that he could only stand there and stare at her. She crossed her arms over her chest and stared back. "Well?" she asked in a voice filled with annoyance when he continued to stare at her and say nothing. "Do I make myself clear?"

Finding his voice, Nolan said, "You most certainly do. However, there's a problem and I consider it a major one."

Those beautiful eyes were razor-sharp and directed at him. "And just what problem is that?"

Now it was he who turned a cutting gaze on her. "I never sent you any flowers. Today or ever."

Find out if Nolan Madaris has finally
met his match in
BEST LAID PLANS
by New York Times *bestselling author*
Brenda Jackson, available March 2018
wherever HQN Books and ebooks are sold.

www.Harlequin.com

COMING NEXT MONTH FROM

Available April 3, 2018

#2581 CLAIM ME, COWBOY

Copper Ridge • by Maisey Yates

Wanted: fake fiancée for a wealthy rancher to teach his father not to play matchmaker. Benefits: your own suite in a rustic mansion and money to secure your baby's future. Rules: deny all sizzling sexual attraction and don't fall in love!

#2582 EXPECTING A SCANDAL

Texas Cattleman's Club: The Impostor • by Joanne Rock

Wealthy trauma surgeon Vaughn Chambers spends his days saving lives and his nights riding the ranch. But when it comes to healing his own heart, he finds solace only in the arms of Abigail Stewart, who's pregnant with another man's baby...

#2583 UPSTAIRS DOWNSTAIRS BABY

Billionaires and Babies • by Cat Schield

Single mom Claire Robbins knows her boss is expected to marry well. Taking up with the housekeeper is just not done—especially if her past catches up to her. Falling for Linc would be the ultimate scandal. But she's never been good at resisting temptation...

#2584 THE LOVE CHILD

Alaskan Oil Barons • by Catherine Mann

When reclusive billionaire rancher Trystan Mikkelson is thrust into the limelight, he needs a media makeover! Image consultant Isabeau Waters guarantees she can turn him into the face of his family's empire. But one night of passion leads to pregnancy, and it could cost them everything.

#2585 THE TEXAN'S WEDDING ESCAPE

Heart of Stone • by Charlene Sands

Rancher Cooper Stone owes the Abbott family a huge debt...and he's been tasked with stopping Lauren Abbott from marrying the wrong man! But how can Lauren trust her feelings when she learns her time with Cooper is a setup?

#2586 HIS BEST FRIEND'S SISTER

First Family of Rodeo • by Sarah M. Anderson

Family scandal chases expectant mother Renee from New York City to Texas. But when rodeo and oil tycoon Oliver, her brother's best friend, agrees to hide her in his Dallas penthouse, sparks fly. Will her scandal ruin him, too?

YOU CAN FIND MORE INFORMATION ON UPCOMING HARLEQUIN® TITLES, FREE EXCERPTS AND MORE AT WWW.HARLEQUIN.COM.

HDCNM0318

Joshua Grayson looked out the window of his office and did
not feel the kind of calm he ought to feel.

He'd moved back to Copper Ridge six months ago from
Seattle, happily trading in a man-made, rectangular skyline
for the natural curve of the mountains.

But right now he doubted anything would decrease the
tension he was feeling from dealing with the fallout of his
father's ridiculous ad. Another attempt by the old man to
make Joshua live the life his father wanted him to.

The only kind of life his father considered successful: a
wife, children.

He couldn't understand why Joshua didn't want the same.

No. That kind of life was for another man, one with
another past and another future. It was not for Joshua. And
that was why he was going to teach his father a lesson.

He wasn't responsible for the ad in a national paper
asking for a wife, till death do them part. But an unsuitable,
temporary wife? Yes. That had been his ad.

He was going to win the game. Once and for all. And the woman he hoped would be his trump card was on her way.

The doorbell rang and he stood up behind his desk. She was here. And she was—he checked his watch—late.

A half smile curved his lips.

Perfect.

He took the stairs two at a time. He was impatient to meet his temporary bride. Impatient to get this plan started so it could end.

He strode across the entryway and jerked the door open. And froze.

The woman standing on his porch was small. And young, just as he'd expected, but… She wore no makeup, which made her look like a damned teenager. Her features were fine and pointed; her dark brown hair hung lank beneath a ragged beanie that looked like it was in the process of unraveling while it sat on her head.

He didn't bother to linger over the rest of the details—her threadbare sweater with too-long sleeves, her tragic skinny jeans—because he was stopped, immobilized really, by the tiny bundle in her arms.

A baby.

His prospective bride had come with a baby.

Well, hell.

Don't miss
CLAIM ME, COWBOY
by New York Times *bestselling author Maisey Yates,*
part of her **COPPER RIDGE** *series!*

Available April 2018 wherever
Harlequin® Desire books and ebooks are sold.

www.Harlequin.com

Want to give in to temptation with
steamy tales of irresistible desire?

Check out **Harlequin® Presents®,
Harlequin® Desire** and
Harlequin® Kimani™ Romance books!

New books available every month!

CONNECT WITH US AT:

Harlequin.com/Community

 Facebook.com/HarlequinBooks

Twitter.com/HarlequinBooks

Instagram.com/HarlequinBooks

Pinterest.com/HarlequinBooks

ReaderService.com

**ROMANCE WHEN
YOU NEED IT**

PGENRE2017

LOVE
Harlequin
romance?

Join our Harlequin community to share your thoughts and connect with other romance readers!

Be the first to find out about promotions, news, and exclusive content!

Sign up for the Harlequin e-newsletter and download a free book from any series at

www.TryHarlequin.com

CONNECT WITH US AT:

Harlequin.com/Community

 Facebook.com/HarlequinBooks

Twitter.com/HarlequinBooks

Instagram.com/HarlequinBooks

Pinterest.com/HarlequinBooks

ReaderService.com

 **HARLEQUIN**®

**ROMANCE WHEN
YOU NEED IT**

HSOCIAL2017